D0464232

J.P. and the Apaches

J.P. and the Apaches

by William Grote

Illustrated by Charles Waterhouse

Meredith Press, New York

First edition

Library of Congress Catalog Card Number: 67-14747
Manufactured in the United States of America for
Meredith Press

To
Sid Fleischman—
with gratitude

Contents

1

The Imp

As far as the eye could see across the great empty desert only two things moved. One was a small gray burro, walking very slowly and raising lazy spurts of dust from its hooves. The other was seated on its back, a brown-skinned, dark-haired, blue-eyed boy who was called J.P. Those initials were short for Juanito Patrick Mendoza O'Flynn.

It was the warm spring morning of April 4, 1866. Desert plants bloomed bashfully after the winter rains. The sight of them and the smell of clean, sharp air made J.P. feel so good that he decided to sing. And sing he did, at the top of his lungs, but not a song that anyone would recognize, because J.P. made it up as he went along.

The sound caused his burro's ears to droop unhappily. Being five times longer than human ears, the burro's ears were also five times as sensitive. And unfortunately J.P. did not have the sweetest voice in the world.

When J.P. noticed the drooping ears he decided to sing even louder. Bravo snorted with disgust. He had been named by J.P.'s father, who decided that this was the most cowardly burro in the Territory of Arizona. Or come to think about it, maybe the smartest. After all, Bravo was still alive even though the Apache Indians loved donkey meat.

Although Bravo could run like a rabbit at the smell of an Indian, most times he seemed barely able to walk. In addition to being a coward, he was also the laziest burro south of the Gila River.

On this bright morning J.P.'s immediate destination was a narrow dry wash lined by Paloverde trees. He and Bravo were an hour out of Fort Bowie, and with each passing second the morning became hotter.

As they approached the smoke trees, J.P.'s heart beat faster. His eyes searched for the rock pile. Yes, they'd been moved since yesterday. He yipped happily. Here was one Apache secret that few Americans knew. He'd made a signal with rocks and it had been answered.

Someone was waiting for him in the secret place.

Sensing J.P.'s happiness, the burro increased his speed all the way to a slow walk. But J.P. didn't really care about speed, he wanted to keep this happy feeling as long as possible. Lately J.P. hadn't had many happy times.

His bright blue eyes caught a cluster of yellow blooms dotting a gaunt organ-pipe cactus. When they reached it he stood up in the leather stirrups to peer into the nest of a desert hawk. The nest was empty. He tried to forget his unhappiness. But even out here on the shining desert the memory of his father throbbed like an ache inside his head.

Suddenly Bravo snorted with alarm and came to an abrupt halt. J.P. felt him shiver.

"Coward," the boy said disdainfully and jumped to the ground. He kicked away a crooked stick. "See? It's just a mesquite branch."

Bravo wasn't sure. Carefully he sniffed the ground, blowing up a cloud of dust after each loud sniff. All right, so it was a stick and not a snake. But it *could* have been a snake. And being careful was the only way to stay alive in that place.

J.P. climbed back into the saddle and they continued on their way.

Not that he really believed his father was dead. Missing, perhaps, but that didn't mean the big, laughing Army scout couldn't return any time now. You might bet he would have a darn good reason why the government survey party he'd led into the Sonora Desert was five weeks overdue. Not thirst nor sickness, nor even the whole Chiricahua tribe of Apaches could get the better of Donegal Dan O'Flynn.

If he could just explain this to his dark-eyed mother when she cried in the late of night. She didn't know that

J.P., his baby sister and brother were usually still awake and listening.

J.P. had a sudden urge to yell.

"Donegal Dan!" he screeched shrilly.

Bravo jumped with alarm. The boy had a very loud voice.

"Donegal Dan the Mountain Man
Showed his teeth and the Indians ran!"

Suddenly he felt like laughing again. It was a spell he had just made up, a spell that told every creature on the desert that he *knew* his father would soon return.

Bravo slowly plodded toward the secret place. J.P. wondered if he was heavy on the burro's back. Suddenly a speckled cactus wren darted across their path. Then a green-striped lizard streaked out from between Bravo's hooves, and suddenly J.P. saw the kit fox.

Only once before had he seen a kit fox in broad daylight. The other long-eared, doglike creature had seemed almost as frightened as this one. He felt its terror as it disappeared into a pile of rocks.

The flapping of wings made him look up. A pair of quail flew heavily overhead toward the far mountains. He wondered about them. This was the nesting season for quail, and only a bad fright would drive both birds away from the nest at the same time. Something was wrong.

"Whoa," he said sharply, tugging the reins. His burro

was glad to stop. It closed its eyes and prepared for a standing-up nap.

"Indians," J.P. whispered, and then slightly louder, "Apaches."

Bravo's eyes flew open. J.P. steered him to a clump of rocks, where the terrorized burro sank to his knees.

"If you know what's good for you," J.P. whispered as he dismounted, "*don't move.*"

Bravo couldn't help but move, not the way he was shivering. J.P. knew it was time for him to hide too. He huddled behind a ten-foot-high saguaro, a tall, spiny cactus with thick branches that stuck out like arms. Saguaros reminded him of old men signaling to each other across the desert. He peered out between thick thorns and waited.

Three Chiricahua Apache braves on horseback approached his hiding place. They rode so close that J.P. could almost hear them breathe. They looked terribly fierce, with long hair, cruel eyes, and paint-streaked faces. J.P. decided it was a raiding party. The face closest to his had a jagged scar across the left cheek, and the brave spoke angrily to the other two. Since J.P.'s father had taught him the Apache tongue, he listened closely.

"My two wives keep me unhappy," complained the brave with the scarred face. "All they want is more horses and more blankets. All the time 'Give me, give me.' I tell you, fellows, they make me want to stay on the warpath and away from home. . . ."

The others clucked their sympathy, and soon their

voices softened with distance. JP.'s heart pumped like the legs of a runaway steer. The Apaches had come so close he could have touched them. That is, if he had wanted to, which he certainly hadn't. Now the danger was about over. All he had to do was wait until the raiding party was out of sight.

But of all crazy times, right then and there the Imp popped into his head. He knew better. He knew he shouldn't do it—but he did it anyway.

He cupped his mouth with both hands and yelped. Not just a plain good-feeling kind of yelp. J.P.'s yelp was like the bark of a coyote that had just stepped on a cactus thorn.

The three Apaches halted. They swung their horses around. That coyote yelp was a signal that Apaches used to call each other from hiding. It meant, "*Help!*"

Behind the saguaro tree J.P. grinned happily. It wasn't often that a twelve-year-old boy got to fool three grown-up Apaches. The brave with the scar stood up in his stirrups and made a coyote yelp of his own. It was just slightly different from J.P.'s yelp, but the difference meant, "*Where are you hiding?*"

J.P. knew better than to answer. Luckily, the Imp was gone now.

Scarface scowled. "You heard?"

The others said they'd heard the yelp. That is, they thought they had. Of course, it might have been the wind . . .

"Not wind," Scarface snarled angrily. He yelped again.

The others shrugged and laughed.

"You think I'm a fool?" Anger made the ugly face even more fierce than before, and the other braves stopped laughing. "We won't leave until I know what made the call."

With a slight kick of his heels he moved his horse toward the saguaro tree.

J.P. swallowed hard. This time he'd gone much too far. Even with the Imp inside his head he should have known not to play around with Chiricahuas. The one with the scar was coming awfully close, and he seemed mean enough to bite a rock in half.

Now the boy was frightened. The Apache was so near that J.P. could see his eyebrows, thick and hairy like black caterpillars. There was only one thing to do. . . .

"*Hoo*," he moaned softly. "*Hoo-hoo* . . ."

It was a fairly good, although somewhat shaky, imitation of an owl. He knew that one thing that terrified Apaches was seeing an owl during daylight, especially since they thought owls to be the ghosts of their dead enemies.

"*Hooo* . . ."

Scarface jerked his horse to a halt.

"*Hooo* . . ."

By now J.P.'s mouth was so dry that he couldn't hoot again if he tried. But it was the Apache's turn to be frightened. He swung his horse around and rejoined his companions. After a few quick looks over their shoulders they galloped off in billowing streamers of dust.

It took a while for the color to return to J.P.'s face. But

he wasn't the only frightened one out there. His little burro was so terrified that he refused to stand up. And not until, after several tries, J.P. managed to whistle a few shaky bars of "O! Susanna" was Bravo convinced that things were back to normal. Then he stood up and yawned as if he hadn't been frightened at all. J.P. wasn't fooled. He knew if he said "Apache" right then, Bravo would flop right down on his knobby knees. But J.P. needed him on his feet, so he was careful not even to whisper that terrible word.

Still breathing hard, the two continued on toward their destination.

2

The Secret Place

It was almost noon when J.P. and Bravo reached the secret place. For something with such a wonderful name it wasn't much to see. From the desert floor below, the hill was only a swelling with a rocky top. But once up there one could look over the edge and see in all directions. J.P. dismounted and led Bravo to the outcropping of sandstone on the hilltop. For a moment he was worried. Then he saw the calico pony tied to a mesquite bush and grinned.

One at a time he examined each squat barrel cactus. Then his eyes moved to the low stands of prickly pears. He saw nothing.

All right, if not behind a cactus bush, then maybe in the sand. Perhaps—yes, over there. There were markings, as if something had dug a long hole in the sand and then covered it again.

J.P.'s blue eyes gleamed. Slowly he approached the spot. With a yell he sat down hard, then leaped to his feet and laughed at what came up from under the sand. It came up spitting. Bravo snorted nervously and trotted away to the far side of the hill.

"I greet you," J.P. said in Apache.

The Indian boy was approximately J.P.'s age. His sand-streaked skin was the color of polished copper, his black, sand-covered hair long and banded tightly across his forehead by a strip of red flannel. Black eyes flashed with anger.

"How did you know?" the Apache boy asked tightly.

"Know what, Natanah?"

"That I hid in the sand."

"I saw the signs you taught me," J.P. replied.

Natanah, which simply meant Cornflower, shook sand from his hair and face. He was still angry, and J.P. understood why. His pride was hurt. Sand-hiding was a secret Apache trick; after their enemies had passed, the warriors would spring up with knife in hand.

Stiffly, Natanah led him to the shade of a rock. J.P. waited for his friend to speak. He was careful not to smile but he wanted to. When he was angry, Natanah looked exactly like a cross little old man.

"I brought you a present," J.P. finally said.

The scowl disappeared. "Let me see."

J.P. took an object from his pocket. It was a paper collar given him by a traveling salesman. Natanah eyed it suspiciously.

"What is that crazy thing?"

J.P. fastened the collar around his neck. "White men wear these when they visit girls."

"Why?" Natanah was puzzled.

"I don't know."

Natanah put out his hand and J.P. dropped the collar into it. A moment later the paper thing was hanging loosely around Natanah's neck. "How do I look?"

"Awful."

Natanah tried to scowl, but his lips puckered, and an instant later he was smiling. J.P. laughed, and soon the two boys bellowed and flopped on their backs and kicked their feet happily in the air.

Watching them, Bravo curled his big lips with disgust. Even a *laughing* Indian gave him the creeps.

Finally, when their belly muscles hurt, the two boys stopped laughing. "I'm glad to see you, *Ish-kay-nay*," said the Apache, using the Chiricahua word for "boy."

"And I'm glad to see you, Natanah."

Natanah hid the paper collar in a special place scooped out beneath a flat rock. The hole contained other presents from J.P.—two brass Army buttons, a tin spur, a small magnet, and a stub of pencil. Natanah was tremendously proud of his collection because for him these items were very rare. Of course, he'd probably never be able to show them to another Apache. If his people knew that he was friendly with a white boy, Natanah would be severely punished. Chiricahuas and white men were deadly enemies.

"We'd better be careful," J.P. said softly. "There's a raiding party close by."

Natanah was startled. "You saw them?"

J.P. explained how he'd fooled the warrior with a scar on his cheek. "Him I know," Natanah said. "He has earned the name of Quick Killer."

"A very strong name."

"Very strong."

"Quick Killer." J.P. shook his head. "That name fits him well."

"Yes. An angry man who has killed many of your people."

Right then as if some cloud had drifted over the sun, the joy of their meeting suddenly seemed spoiled.

"Natanah, how would your people punish you if they found us together?"

"I'm not sure." The Apache boy frowned. "Maybe they would not let me become a warrior."

That was serious punishment, J.P. knew. Natanah lived for the day when he would become a warrior.

"And you, Ish-kay-nay? What would happen to you?"

J.P. said he wasn't sure either. But it would certainly cause a loud ruckus at Fort Bowie. Maybe his father would even lose his job as an Army scout. But if they were careful, no one need ever know about them. . . .

Alone in the shade of the rock outcropping, they sat side by side and talked of many things. They talked about the days before 1862, when the Apaches and white men were friends, until at Apache Pass a terrible mistake was made and some of the relatives of the great chief, Cochise, were killed by American soldiers. Since then the Chiricahua, the tribe to which Natanah belonged, had been at war with every white in the whole southern part of the Arizona Territory.

After talking ran down, the boys wrestled. They grunted and squirmed and tugged and pushed. Since neither was really stronger then the other, they finally flopped on their backs like drowning fish and gulped for air. From far away, J.P.'s burro watched nervously.

The Apache boy grinned at Bravo. "That one would be good to eat."

Bravo's ears flattened. He walked farther away and Natanah blinked with surprise.

"Can that thing understand talk?" he asked J.P.

"I don't know. But sometimes I wonder if he's a burro or just a lazy old witch."

"You'd be happier with a pony, Ish-kay-nay."

J.P. nodded. "My father promised that someday he'd get me a horse. Now I'm not sure he ever will. . . ."

Natanah looked at him strangely. "You are sad, Ish-kay-nay?"

"I . . . guess so."

"Why?"

J.P. told him how his father had failed to return from the Sonora Desert. Natanah listened quietly and then said, "I will ask if any of our warriors have recently fought with white men on the southern desert. Especially will I try to learn of the long-haired scout whom you call your father. When next we meet perhaps I'll know."

"Thank you, Natanah." But J.P. suddenly wondered how he'd feel toward his friend if the Apaches *had* killed his father.

"The day is still young," Natanah said suddenly. "Come, we'll hunt."

And hunt they did—for horned toads. After each had found one, they drew a circle on the sand and raced the fierce-looking lizards. Natanah's crossed the line first and the Apache boy danced with glee.

The day wore on. Time passed very quickly for the two boys, who seemed constantly to find another question to ask the other. J.P. explained about reading and writing. Drawing letters on the sand, he showed Natanah how white men could talk by making marks on paper.

They discussed the way they'd met. J.P. had found Natanah on the ground with a sprained ankle after the Indian's pony had tripped in a prairie-dog hole. J.P. had brought him water and food, and talked with him in his own language. Because they were of the same age although from different worlds, their friendship was fed by curiosity. At each meeting that curiosity became stronger, and so did their understanding of each other.

The sun was lowering in the western sky when Natanah saw Quick Killer's raiding party on the desert below. The Indian boy cautioned J.P. to silence. Side by side on the rim rocks they watched the three warriors pass.

"They've stolen two horses," Natanah whispered proudly.

J.P. nodded. There was no sense telling him that white men thought stealing to be wrong. Stealing was a way of life with the Apaches.

Natanah finally decided it was time for him to leave. He and J.P. agreed to meet again in three days.

"Good-bye, Ish-kay-nay," the Apache boy said fondly.

"Good-bye, Natanah. And remember to ask about my father. . . ."

Cornflower sped away on his pony. J.P. watched awhile, then, with a feeling of tired happiness, climbed on Bravo's back and aimed him homeward.

J.P.'s mother was very upset.

"You know it's dangerous to go that far from the fort," she said angrily. "Suppose the Indians found you."

J.P. knew she was right to think that way. The Chiricahuas under the leadership of Cochise were so fierce that only a series of Army forts, of which Fort Bowie was one, made it possible for white men to remain in the area. The adobe hut in which J.P.'s family lived was part of a small cluster of settlers' houses near the main Fort Bowie gate. Living in the shadow of the Sixth Cavalry was fairly safe.

But there wasn't much safety on the desert. And, of course, his mother didn't know about his black-haired friend. . . .

"Juanito, you promised never to go that far from home."

"I'm sorry, Mamá." And he was, because he truly loved his mother. Only his need to learn about his father had made him disobey her. Or at least so he told himself.

"I'll have to punish you, Juanito."

Bed without supper. Oh well, things could be worse. J.P. climbed under the down covers near the barred square hole that served them as a window. From his bed he could see stars above. His baby sister Maria cried fitfully, and his brother Pepe, who was nearly four years old, snored like a man. Soon J.P. heard his mother go to bed. He pulled the pillow around his ears so that tonight he wouldn't hear her cry.

He thought about this morning, when the Imp popped into his head. It was a feeling hard to describe—sort of like frozen laughter. When it was in his head he could almost understand the feelings of wild animals and birds. Sometimes it made him do crazy things, like when he coyote-yelped those three Apaches.

J.P. used to worry about the Imp, until he told his father about it and Donegal Dan proudly said it was "the little people in your head, me bucko." Donegal Dan told him that now and then the "little people" came into every Irishman's head—even when they were only half Irish. That's what made Irishmen different from everyone else. He said that when used right, the Imp was a blessing. So although J.P. was never sure whether or not he used it right, he stopped worrying about the thing. Anything his father thought all right was certainly fine with him too.

And on that happy thought he fell asleep. When he awakened a bell was tolling somewhere close. He sat up and saw that it was still dark outside. From the distance he heard rifle shots.

"An Apache raid," his mother whispered in the darkness. "Probably at the corral." Her voice grew angry. "Cochise's people are becoming more daring all the time. Now they're not even afraid of our soldiers."

An exaggeration, J.P. thought excitedly. It was probably only a small raid. Just two or three warriors sneaking into the settlers' corral for horses. Suddenly he remembered that he'd left Bravo in the corral. The memory made him leap out to the floor.

"Where are you going?" his mother asked.

"To Bravo, Mamá. He's in the corral."

"Back in that bed!"

"But—"

"I said back!"

Almost angrily J.P. crawled under the covers again. If the Apaches stole Bravo and ate him, that would be Mamacita's fault.

All of a sudden, there was a loud "*Hee-aww! Hee-aww!*"

Baby sister cried out at the loud, rusty-gate sound. Little

brother yelled angrily. Mamá spoke fiercely, and J.P. fell back against his pillow laughing.

Because pressed against the barred window opening was a whitish, ugly face. This was one burro who had absolutely no intention of becoming part of an Apache stew.

3

Sioux Talk and Mr. Long

The next night J.P. had nightmares. Mostly they were about his father and what could have happened to him on the Sonora Desert. He was very glad when the light of day awakened him.

Two more days and he'd be back at the secret place. He hoped he could somehow wait that long. . . .

The family ate a hearty breakfast of flapjacks and canned peaches—as an Army employee, J.P.'s father was allowed to purchase food from the fort commissary. Some of their food was obtained in exchange for eggs freshly laid by eighteen loudly cackling hens penned up in the yard. During cool weather those chickens were good for at least a dozen eggs per day.

It was J.P.'s job to gather the eggs and barter with the post mess sergeant, so after breakfast he went out to rob the hens. While placing the loot into a straw basket, under the bored eyes of Bravo, who was tied to a stake nearby, he heard the rattle of an approaching surrey.

Quickly he looked up. The only surrey at Fort Bowie was owned by the wife of Colonel Blunt, commander of the post. J.P.—or more properly, Bravo—had had a few bad run-ins with the lady.

He saw Mrs. Blunt sitting next to the driver, her face strong and pretty in a proud sort of way. The man driving the single-horse wagon wore fringed buckskin clothing. He had shoulder-length hair and moustaches so thick and stiff that J.P. wondered if a boy his size could hang on without making them bend. This strange person called himself Winchester Q. Long, and he claimed to be a famous mountain man and scout. Without really knowing why, J.P. doubted that he was. Maybe because, unlike his father who was quiet and simply dressed, this man always made a big fuss about himself.

Politely J.P. nodded to the Colonel's wife. She smiled briefly and nodded back. Then she saw Bravo and her smile disappeared like the sun behind a thundercloud.

"That terrible beast," she snapped.

"Yes, ma'am," agreed Mr. Long.

"Gets loose and eats my flowers."

"Indeed? Then the burro hasn't got sense. If he did he'd eat your weeds"—a sideways wink at J.P.—"just to please you, ma'am."

The Colonel's wife glanced sharply at Mr. Long to see if he were making fun of her. J.P. decided he was. The boy turned away to hide his grin, and a moment later Mrs. Blunt and the would-be scout entered the O'Flynn hut to talk with his mother.

Of course it was impolite to eavesdrop, but he found the temptation hard to resist. Usually each morning the Colonel's wife rode her surrey out on the desert. She was always guarded against Indian attacks by four mounted troopers. J.P. wondered why she'd change her routine today. Why was the most important woman at Fort Bowie visiting his mother?

Only one way to find out, he decided: by listening at the window.

"And we're planning a tea for the officers' wives," said the voice of Mrs. Blunt. "I wondered if you would like to cook some tamales for us. Your tamales are famous, Mrs. O'Flynn, and we know you can use the money. Especially since your husband's death–"

"Excuse me," said J.P.'s mother firmly, "but my husband is not dead. Unless you have heard something I haven't."

"Not officially, no."

"And we do not need the money, *señora*. However, to please you I will make tamales."

"Thank you. And about your husband, Mrs. O'Flynn. I'm sorry if I said anything wrong. But Mr. Long here is a famous scout and he says–"

"Allow me to explain, madam," said the deep, smooth voice of Winchester Q. Long. "Sometimes it's easier to face the truth than to keep hoping. I've had years of experience, ma'am. That's why I say it is possible your husband met an untimely end. Perhaps because of hostile savages, or maybe even through an error of his own . . ."

J.P. covered his ears. He didn't want to hear what the man was saying. Didn't want to believe what he'd already heard. There was just one quick way to make Mr. Long stop talking.

He untied Bravo and led his burro to the opening in the adobe wall.

"Bray," whispered J.P. as he pulled a small hair in Bravo's tail.

"*Hee-aww.*"

"Louder!"

Bravo strained. "HEE-AWW. HEE-AWW . . . !"

The deep, smooth voice broke off. There was a harsh cry from Mrs. Blunt. A moment later Mamacita O'Flynn came flying from the hut.

"For shame, Juanito! To let that jackass make so much noise when the Colonel's wife is inside! Take him away, you understand?"

"Yes, Mamá." But J.P. sensed that although her words were harsh, deep in her eyes there lay understanding. Ah . . . Mamacita knew why he'd caused the disturbance.

He returned to the hens to gather more eggs. After a while he heard footsteps. When he looked up, Winchester Long was towering over him. This close the man's eyes were dark and shiny, his moustachioed mouth was curved in a smile.

"You gave the great lady quite a scare, boy."

J.P. looked away. "I'm sorry–I guess."

"Lifted *me* right out of my chair, too." He squinted at Bravo. "He's got a powerful throat to be so small."

J.P. couldn't help but smile. They stood grinning at each other, a large long-haired man and a sun-browned boy of twelve.

"By the way, boy. I hear your father prospected before coming here. That true?"

J.P. nodded.

"He ever find gold?"

J.P. picked up another egg and placed it in the straw basket.

"Well?"

"Maybe yes, maybe no." J.P. mumbled his answer; it really wasn't anyone else's business.

"That mean you ain't talking?"

"Guess it does–sir."

Winchester Long plucked at his moustache as if playing a harp. "Just asked out of curiosity, boy. Making conversation, that's all. One famous old scout to the son of another. Of course you've heard of me. Winchester Q. Long?"

"Yes, sir. I sure have."

The long-haired man looked pleased. "From your dad?"

"Er–nope."

"Then where?"

J.P. decided not to say. He'd heard about him, all right, mostly from soldiers. Especially those who had played cards with the man and had lost a month's pay to him. To them the fellow was a professional cardsharp. Yet J.P. couldn't help liking Mr. Long, although something told him it would be best not to get too friendly. "Guess I'd better take these eggs to the mess hall now."

"How come?"

"We trade them for provisions."

"Good idea. Eggs are scarce around here, and those you've got look mighty tempting." One hand flicked into his pocket to come out holding a thick roll of green bills. "I've always been an egg lover, ever since my yearling days on the farm. How's about selling them to me?"

J.P. blinked at the thick roll of money. Why, there seemed as much as *fifty dollars!* He swallowed hard. "Afraid I can't, sir. They're promised to the mess sergeant."

The man held out the money long enough to make J.P.'s eyes grow as round as two grindstones. Then, with a shrug, he made the bills disappear into his pocket. "Sure your dad never mentioned me, boy?"

"Sure, sir."

"Well, maybe because I done most of my scouting in the Dakota country. Fought with the Sioux, and I'll tell you something. Them Sioux are so mean they make your Apaches seem like sissies in blue velvet pants."

J.P. still didn't believe the man. He wasn't going to say

so, and he could have picked up his basket, waved good-bye, and moved on. Except that right then a small bit of the Imp popped into his head.

"Seems I heard some Sioux talk once," he said.

Mr. Long's dark eyes narrowed. "That so?"

"I think it went like this . . ." And J.P. made up words that came out sounding like a bullfrog with hiccups.

Winchester Long squinted. "How's that again?"

"*Haba-daba-kaba-op*," J.P. repeated.

The man tugged his moustaches, thought a moment, and nodded. "Sounds like Sioux, all right."

The boy grinned.

"But I don't understand it," the long-haired man added quickly. "Because, boy, your accent's all wrong."

He laughed, and J.P. laughed with him, and between them was the sudden understanding that each had joshed the other. Then the man was holding out a five-dollar bill. "Guess I can spare this for the language lesson."

J.P. stopped laughing and gulped. But then he shook his head. "Afraid I can't take it, sir."

"How come?"

"My father wouldn't like me taking money I hadn't earned."

"Good upbringing, I'd say. But maybe there's a way you can earn it."

"Sir?"

The man looked down at his fingernails and blew on them gently. "You see, I like to socialize. Like to get together with friends and talk, maybe sometimes play a friendly game of cards. But these soldier boys, now. Some of them's got the foolish idea that my card playing is peculiar. In fact, it's getting downright hard for me to find a sociable card game."

"I've heard that, sir."

"Heard?" Winchester Long frowned. "Hmm. But about this five-dollar bill . . ."

Again J.P. swallowed hard. It was an *awful* lot of cash.

"I'll gladly give it to you, boy. All you've got to do for me is let the soldiers hear that your dad talked about Winchester Long. You know, how he knew me for a mountain man and a trusty Indian scout? Folks around here think a heap of your dad. If you was to let 'em think I was his friend, why, they might even be glad to have me socialize with 'em."

"And play cards?"

"And play a friendly game, that's right. You willing to do that for five dollars?"

"Yes, sir."

Winchester Long grinned happily.

"Soon as my father gets back, sir. And soon after that as he says it's all right."

For a moment Mr. Long looked angry. Then, in that low voice, he said, "You mean *if* he gets back, boy?"

"No, sir. *When* he gets back."

A deep sigh. Then the man who liked to play cards with

the soldiers walked back toward the adobe hut. J.P. watched him go.

And in his mind the memory of that five-dollar bill grew fainter and fainter, and every minute that it faded it seemed to hurt.

4

A Fine Morning

An hour later J.P. approached the gate to Fort Bowie with his basket of eggs. Suddenly, behind him sounded the rattle, squeak, and clatter of the government mail coach arriving from Tucson. He leaped aside so fast he almost lost his eggs. As the four-horse team galloped past, the driver waved.

"Hi, J.P.!"

J.P. waved back at the man whose red beard shone brightly in the morning sun. Tom Bowman was usually known by his Indian name of Firechin. As the government mail agent, he ran the stage line from Fort Bowie to Tucson, a distance of almost one hundred miles. Lately the

Indian attacks had been so bad that those of his drivers who weren't wounded had just plain quit. Now Firechin Tom was driving the stage himself.

As he approached the stage station, J.P. passed some Pima scouts squatting on the ground. He wondered what they'd think if they knew he was friends with an Apache. Then Firechin Tom dropped a hand on J.P.'s shoulder while his leathery face crinkled with pleasure.

"Great seeing you again, J.P."

"Same here, Tom. What kind of trip'd you have?"

"Like always. Cochise's braves chased us four different times. One of these days they're going to catch us, too. That'll mean the end of the stage line." He grinned. "And me too, I guess."

J.P. had heard the Firechin Tom carried at least a dozen arrow marks and bullet nicks on his body. Only his stubbornness and courage kept him driving through Apache country.

"Any word on your dad?"

J.P. said No, and the leathery face softened.

"Haven't given up hope, have you?"

"Not me," replied J.P. "Although some folks around here have."

"Sure. There are gloomy cusses about everywhere. Shucks, Donegal Dan'll make it back if anyone can." He ruffled J.P.'s hair. "I'll come by to see you and your mom before I leave for Tucson. Tell her I've brought word from her brother."

"Right, Tom. We'll be glad to see you."

J.P. continued toward the mess hall. Suddenly a noise from behind made him turn.

There stood Bravo with a piece of the tie-up rope still trailing from his neck.

"Scat!" J.P. ordered angrily. "Go on–get *home*."

Bravo drew back his ears. His feelings were hurt. With a "to-heck-with-you" look on his long face he turned and walked slowly back toward the gate. *Pain in the neck*, J.P. thought. That crazy burro would never learn. . . .

He walked slowly. The interior of Fort Bowie always excited him; it was filled with so many different sounds. The creaking wheels of supply wagons, the howling of mule drivers, and the tramp of feet on the dusty parade ground where a column of men was drilling in the hot sun.

He passed Officer's Row and walked faster at sight of the Colonel's plank house fronted by a colorful flower garden. Then he reached the large wooden mess hall and entered by the rear door.

"Sergeant Schultz?"

A giant of a man wearing a floppy trooper's hat lumbered into view. His tremendous stomach stuck out behind a white apron like a hill of snow, and the left sleeve of his uniform shirt glistened brightly with rank and service stripes. "That you, O'Flynn?" asked the giant in a surprisingly mild voice.

"Me." J.P. held up his basket toward Master Sergeant

Herman "Big Bull" Schultz. Big Bull was in charge of the Sixth Cavalry mess hall, and he peered slyly into the basket.

"What are they, O'Flynn?"

"Eggs, of course."

"No fooling." He picked one up. "Pigeons'?"

"Of course not. They're from–"

"Cactus wrens?"

"No, from our . . ."

"Hummingbirds."

". . . chickens. The same size eggs as always, Sergeant."

"Well, maybe so." Blue eyes twinkled from a crinkled, weather-beaten face. "Let's see. One, two, three . . ." He counted the eggs slowly, pretending they were so small he had trouble finding them. "A dozen, if a man's got good eyes. Maybe enough for the Colonel's breakfast–providing he ain't too hungry. What you want for them?"

"Three–no, four loaves of bread," J.P. said quickly.

"Hmmm. Then hold out your basket."

J.P. did so, and in two scoops a huge hand removed the eggs. Then a returning hand dropped in four loaves of bread. "Heard anything 'bout your father?"

"I'm afraid not yet."

A slab of butter fell into the basket. "How long is he overdue?"

"Five weeks, Sergeant." A can of peaches followed the butter.

"Bad country out there. But your dad's smart." A cloth-wrapped ham was jammed beneath J.P.'s arm. "He'll make it back if anyone does." J.P.'s shirt was pulled forward and a huge load of hard candies dropped inside. "This here's leavings from a birthday party. Surplus, you might say."

"Sergeant," said J.P., beginning to perspire slightly.

"Hush up." Four oranges joined the candy in the front of his shirt.

"Sergeant," J.P. said imploringly. "I don't believe I can hold any more."

Gentle eyes gleamed. "Not even this?"

Big Bull was holding a corked bottle of soda pop. J.P.'s mouth watered. It was more than a year since he'd tasted cream soda. "Well, maybe if it was stuck in my belt . . ."

J.P. grunted as his belt became so tight he could hardly breathe. "Thank you, Sergeant. You're very kind."

"Like to see a growing boy eat. Myself, I never got enough chow when I was small."

Seeing him now made that hard to believe. J.P. grinned, and the big sergeant patted his stomach and smiled. Then suddenly J.P. heard a peculiar sound, a noise that made his joy at the sergeant's generosity melt like midsummer snow.

"*Hee-aww. Hee-aww!*"

"Sergeant," J.P. said. "I'm afraid . . ."

"I hear it." Big Bull Schultz's weather-beaten face creased until it looked like a pool of dried mud. "Sounds like your burro."

"I'm afraid so."

"Loose again."

"Yes, sir."

"Like last time."

"Sorry . . ."

"When he came in the back door. Ate the officers' Sunday salad—remember?"

"I remember."

"Can't let it happen again."

"No, sir."

Big Bull reached up and removed a giant black skillet from an overhanging hook. J.P. gulped. "What—what are you going to do?"

"Head him off." With giant strides the sergeant began walking toward the door. "And if that don't work, I'll paddle him."

J.P. tried to follow the huge man at a run, but he was too heavily loaded to move fast. When Bravo's rusty-door screeches grew louder, J.P. reluctantly emptied his belt and shirt and placed his basket on the kitchen floor. There was little chance that Big Bull Schultz would be this generous again today. Not after chasing Bravo away from the kitchen. But some things in life were more important even than ham and oranges and—*cream soda?*

J.P. rushed into the sunlight and found the situation worse than he had imagined. It was Bravo all right. But above his braying trilled another sound, the shrill, angry voice of Mrs. Blunt. And sure enough, Bravo was standing squarely in the middle of her flower garden. One white dahlia still hung from his hairy upper lip.

"Ugly, flower-eating beast!" The Colonel's wife shook a broom at Bravo's long face. "Hear me? Out, I say!"

The broom whished past the burro's head. It didn't really come close, but the wind scared him.

"*Hee-aww!*"

Big Bull Schultz stopped and turned away. When J.P. reached him the sergeant shook his head. "Won't need this," he said, holding up the skillet. "That donkey's in bad enough trouble. Mrs. Blunt, she's a real flower-loving lady."

J.P. ran to the garden. "Out of there, Bravo," he yelled.

"Immediately—*please*." Tears glistened in the woman's eyes.

Now Bravo was worried—worried enough to do what every self-respecting burro does when things are going badly. He sat down.

As donkeys go, he wasn't very big, yet his stern end somehow managed to cover most of the flowers in Mrs. Blunt's small garden. Angry tears flowed down her cheeks. J.P. felt sorry for her, but in all that confusion he just could not make Bravo obey him. At that moment Mr. Winchester Q. Long came striding along, hair flowing like wings behind his head.

"My dear lady," he said with a deep bow. "If I can be of service . . ."

"Get that creature out of there!"

"It will be my pleasure to rid you of this hairy scourge." He grabbed the bit of rope around Bravo's neck and tugged, but it was like trying to rip out a tree stump.

"Don't fret, ma'am," said Mr. Long, breathing hard. Again he tugged at the rope. Again Bravo refused to move.

"*Please,*" J.P. begged the burro.

Bravo didn't exactly shake his head, but he might as well have. He blinked his eyes and showed yellow teeth. J.P. became angry; this fool burro was making an idiot of him.

Puffing, Winchester Long gave up. "Sorry, ma'am. He's —heavier than—I thought."

The unhappy lady sobbed, J.P. yelled threats, and a crowd began to gather. Several soldiers offered suggestions, not all of which were gentle. Then a tall figure strode

through the crowd and Firechin Tom grinned down at the boy.

"He just won't listen to me, Tom," said J.P. desperately.

Firechin Tom listened to the yells, to Mrs. Blunt's weeping, then he squared his broad shoulders and stepped close to the squatting donkey.

"Burro," he said calmly, and two long ears turned suddenly in his direction. "You're causing an awful fuss. Why, these flowers aren't even good for you. They're too full of

seeds. Why don't you just stand up and skedaddle? Come on, now. Up."

Silence from the crowd as they watched and waited. The long ears twitched. Then Bravo rose to his feet, flicked his tail disdainfully, and walked slowly toward the stockade gate.

"Well, bust my britches," whispered Winchester Long.

Mrs. Blunt stared unbelievingly. "Thank you very much," she said to Firechin Tom. "But—did it really understand you?"

"I don't hardly think so," grinned the stage driver. "It's just that with all this yelling you folks forgot something important."

"What's that?" asked J.P., still angry.

"Appealing to his dignity. A donkey's got more dignity than anything else. Even more than stubbornness." He placed a firm hand on J.P.'s arm and led him away from the departing crowd.

"From now on better keep that burro tied," the stage driver suggested gently.

"I try, Tom. Each time he chews the rope."

"Maybe I can bring a length of chain from Tucson."

"You think so?"

"Sure. A man can get anything in Tucson. You never seen the likes of that place in your life. Seems like everyone there is selling to the Army Quartermaster. Maybe someday I'll take you to visit your uncle. He's a big man in Tucson."

J.P. said he'd like to visit his mother's brother, but he wasn't hankering to visit Tucson. As a future desert scout, towns gave him the whim-whams.

"Just as well," Tom replied. "The ride to Tucson's getting more dangerous all the time. I don't think Cochise will rest until he's driven every white man from the Territory."

"Can't hardly blame him," J.P. replied. "This was Apache land before the whites came."

"Maybe yes and maybe no. There are them who says the Apaches stole it from other tribes. Just like they steal everything else." Firechin Tom scowled. "One of these days I'd like to meet up with old Cochise. I'd put it to him straight. 'Old Man, I'm tired of running from your braves. Let's have it over with here and now. Either kill me, or from here out leave me and my driver alone."

"Would you really be that brave?"

Firechin Tom laughed, and his red beard wagged like a chipmunk's tail. "Maybe yes, maybe no. Bravery's something a man can't be sure about until the time comes." He pointed at Winchester Q. Long, walking ahead of them. "Of course, then there are men like him. Someone who thinks himself brave *all* the time."

J.P. nodded. "He calls himself a scout."

"Could be—but I doubt it."

"You don't think he's brave as he says?"

"Nope, except maybe at a card table. To my nose he has

the smell of a man fast to make a dollar. And probably not too fussy how."

The boy and the red-bearded man parted with a friendly good-bye. J.P. turned toward home, but a few seconds later his feet moved in another direction, and he soon found himself back at the big mess hall. By the rear door he cleared his throat loudly. No one inside seemed to hear.

He cleared it again, this time loud enough to make some passing troopers turn and stare at him. Then he walked slowly around the building, now and then jumping up high so that anyone inside might see him through the windows.

But no one did. Well, then, he decided, this was probably his time to be brave. Taking a deep breath, J.P. walked into the mess hall.

"Sergeant . . . Schultz?" His voice sounded shaky.

"Wondered when you'd come back!"

J.P. spun around, and the giant in the floppy hat was standing behind him in the doorway.

"Want something, O'Flynn?"

J.P. nodded.

"Like what?"

"Er . . . my bread."

"Nothing else?"

"Er . . ." Why was it so darn hard not to sound greedy? "Seems I *did* leave a few things on the floor."

"See them now?"

"Nope."

"Then they're gone."

"For good?"

" 'Fraid so, O'Flynn."

Gone! Suddenly J.P. became angry. "Then I'll take back my eggs."

A smile broke out on the creased face. "You're a pretty spunky kid. But don't worry. I just came back from delivering that stuff to your house."

J.P. said meekly, "All of it, Sergeant?"

"All of it."

"Including . . . the cream soda?"

"That too."

J.P. grinned. "Thank you again."

As he was walking home, a terrible thought hit him. What if his little brother Pepe found that cream soda? He broke into a run.

Inside the adobe hut he drew himself up sharply. Pepe was drinking cream soda, all right. But so was his baby sister. And Mamacita too!

Her eyes sparkled. "Your bottle is over there, Juanito. The good sergeant brought enough cream soda for us all."

Which meant it had turned out to be a pretty fine morning.

5

News of Donegal Dan

The day on which J.P. was again to meet Natanah seemed determined never to come. But come it finally did, and it was a day well worth waiting for.

It started with a sword-sharp morning, bright and shimmering with the exciting feel of spring. His mother warned him against going too far into the desert. He hated to disobey her, but surely she would forgive him when she knew why. Today he hoped to hear news about his father.

He mounted Bravo and aimed him toward the outside trail. But suddenly he jerked the burro to a halt. Mrs. Blunt's surrey, surrounded by her honor guard of four mounted troopers, rattled through the Fort Bowie gateway. In the dust raised by her wheels the Colonel's wife failed to see the boy and burro.

On the way to the secret place J.P. laughed at a chattering blue jay that tried to pluck a hair from Bravo's tail. Then a red-thatched woodpecker chirruped scoldingly at the boy as it darted from a cholla hole. And there were the cactus flowers—the purple buds of the fishhooks, and yellow clusters on the upper horns of the staghorn cholla.

How he loved this place of desolation! There were the hills banded with shifting colors, the ancient brown mountains ringing the horizon on all sides, the pungent smell of sage, of creosote and juniper bushes. J.P. doubted that there was a more beautiful place than this anywhere in the world.

Shortly before noon they reached the secret place. Once more Natanah was nowhere to be seen, but J.P. knew his friend was close. The calico pony stood roped to a creosote bush. When J.P. leaped to the ground, Bravo wrinkled his broad nostrils and strode stiff-leggedly away from the Indian pony smell.

All right, thought J.P. Now where was his fierce friend, Cornflower? His eyes darted quickly over the sand, but this time there were no unusual signs. Slowly he walked near the sandstone rocks and again failed to find a single clue to Natanah's location.

That meant only one thing. The Apache was hiding elsewhere than in the secret place. Not exactly fair, perhaps. But J.P. knew it was important for Natanah's pride that this time he win the game of hide-and-seek.

So he sat on a rock to wait . . . and was suddenly grabbed around the neck from behind. For one instant the arm tightened. Then the pressure loosened and Natanah stood before him grinning broadly.

"I could have killed you," Cornflower announced happily.

"You could have, all right. Where were you hiding?"

Natanah pointed between two brown rocks.

"But I looked there," J.P. complained.

Natanah slid between the rocks and curled himself into a ball. His skin color blended perfectly with the color of the rocks. He was just about invisible.

"You win," J.P. said with a rueful grin.

"My father would be proud of me," Natanah said happily. "Soon I begin training as a warrior. He'll be surprised at what I've already learned."

The idea of warrior training interested J.P. greatly. "How long do you train to become a warrior?"

"Until I'm *tin-sah-tah-hay*, fourteen years old. That means two years of very hard work."

"Doing what?"

"First, special exercises to make me strong. Like rising before the sun and running to the top of a high mountain while carrying heavy rocks. Then I'll learn to go three days and nights without sleeping. I will also fight trees, trying to uproot the small ones. Later I'll burn dry sage on my skin without flinching."

"On your skin?" J.P. asked dubiously.

"Yes. To prove I can stand pain."

J.P. wondered if his friend wasn't overdoing things a little. "Cooked Cornflower," he said and laughed at the idea.

Natanah suddenly became ferocious. "That is a name I cannot help. I told you, it was given me by my mother. Someday I will earn a better one!"

"Like what?"

"Like Strangler-of-Big-Mouthed-Boy-from-Fort-Bowie." It was Natanah's turn to laugh.

J.P. took something from his pocket. "I brought you another present."

Natanah examined it critically; it was a curved piece of glass. "What does it do?"

"See?" J.P. held it before his eye so Natanah could see it magnify.

"It gives you the eye of a cow."

"Something else it does." J.P. held it over Natanah's arm and brought the sun's rays to a sharp focus.

"Ouch!" Natanah yanked his arm away and J.P. grinned.

"Like burning sage," the white boy said.

"You tricked me, Ish-kay-nay."

Natanah was becoming angry again and J.P. decided to

change the subject. "What else will you do to become a warrior?"

"Learn to fight! Learn to shoot a stolen rifle, to use the bow and arrow, the club and bone-handled knife. After that I shall be a Chiricahua warrior. I will kill many enemies!"

J.P. drew an aimless circle with his finger on the sand. "You'll be a warrior and I'll be a desert scout. Maybe we'll meet out here someday. Then you'll try to kill me."

"I will never try to kill you, Ish-kay-nay. Forever you'll be my friend."

J.P. nodded. Things would be like that with him too. "Natanah?"

"Yes?"

"I've waited all morning for you to talk about my father."

Natanah nodded and scowled at the glittering sand. "And I have wanted not to talk. Maybe I have news, Ish-kay-nay."

"Bad news?" There was a sudden tightness in J.P.'s throat.

"Maybe. Last night the warriors spoke around the campfire about their raids and fights. Some have just returned from the Mexican desert. There they attacked a party of Americans. One of these was a yellow-haired American with blue eyes who spoke Apache."

It sounded exactly like Donegal Dan. "What happened to him, Natanah?"

"He fought bravely."

"Of course."

"But he was wounded."

J.P. pressed his lips together. "Badly?"

"It is not known, only that he was bleeding. The others were killed, and only the yellow-haired one escaped, mostly because he knew Apache ways of fighting. He was searched for but not found."

Suddenly there was darkness in J.P.'s mind. Wounded and alone, even Donegal Dan couldn't make it back to Fort Bowie. Maybe his wonderful, laughing father was dead after all. . . .

He fought against the stinging in his eyes. He didn't want Natanah to see him cry. But his eyes burned so badly he had to turn away. Until Natanah said, "Look, Ish-kay-nay. We are being watched."

Side by side on the brown rock were two fat kangaroo rats. They sat on their haunches like plump little men, watching the boys. Their black, protruding eyes blinked, and from deep in their throats came a drumming sound. Black noses wrinkled at the human smell. Like two overfed beggars they sat until even J.P. was forced to laugh. At that sound the rats suddenly disappeared.

"It is good to hear you laugh again, Ish-kay-nay. One grieves much for a father. Yours must have been very fine."

J.P. told Natanah about his father. The Indian boy listened with silent understanding; he too loved his father.

"Yes, I would be very sad if my father disappeared," Natanah admitted. "You see, when one's father dies it is hard to become a warrior. A boy's father is also his teacher."

J.P. nodded sadly. Donegal Dan had been training him in the secrets of desert scouting. . . .

Natanah's calico pony snorted with boredom. Bravo showed his contempt for the calico by pulling back his upper lip and displaying yellow teeth. That made Natanah chuckle.

"At least the burro is good for laughs," Natanah said.

J.P. smiled. "I've had him since my eighth birthday. At first he was fun to ride. Now he's grown older and more lazy. I'd prefer a horse. In fact, my father was going to get me one soon. But now . . ."

Natanah gripped J.P.'s hand and led him to the calico pony. "See my saddle," he said proudly. "The frame is of cottonwood, the seat of deer hide. It is stretched over the frame and laced tightly into place."

"Was this horse stolen?"

"No. He was captured wild by my father's brother and given to me." Natanah's eyes gleamed at the memory. "Would you like to ride my pony?"

J.P.'s heart leaped. "If you think I can."

"Yes. After I show you how to use his rope."

Natanah showed J.P. how to guide the pony. J.P. quickly worked his way up to the pony's back. The calico skittered slightly from side to side, but Natanah's voice soon calmed the sensitive animal. Bravo watched closely. He seemed unable to believe his eyes.

"Now?" J.P. asked.

"Now."

A slight nudge of J.P.'s heel and the pony bounded forward. Instantly the wind was singing in the boy's ears. But not so loudly that he did not hear behind him:

"*Hee-aww*," brayed in a tone of angry surprise.

The pony bounded down the slope of the hill and across the desert floor. J.P. held tightly with his legs and hands. A wonderful excitement surged in his throat. Never before had he ridden so fast.

Once he turned his head and saw the hill as a small mound far behind him. He started to turn the pony around, but the excitement was too strong to turn back yet.

Faster and faster he rode, almost as if to reach the great gray mountains near the horizon. Suddenly, through eyes slitted against the wind, J.P. saw that he was riding directly toward a large band of Apache warriors. He was so close he could see the red dabs of their hair bands. Instinctively he jerked the rawhide rope hard, almost making the pony skid in a sharp left turn. He jabbed with his heels. The pony's head flattened forward.

J.P. raced back toward Natanah. Once he looked behind to see if the Apaches were following, but all he saw was the cloud of dust raised by the pony's hooves. He reached the secret place, stopped the pony, and leaped off.

"Chiricahuas," he told Natanah breathlessly. "Down there."

"They saw you?"

J.P. nodded.

"Bad." Natanah scowled. "Wait here."

He leaped on the pony's back and disappeared over the rim of the hill.

"Down," J.P. told Bravo. "Apaches coming."

Until he heard that, Bravo was stiff-eared with anger. How dare his young master ride off on that skinny, smelly pony? But when he heard the dreaded word "Apache," the burro forgot his pride. In fact he almost tripped in his hurry to flatten himself against the ground.

Side by side they waited. Before J.P.'s eyes a line of red ants marched with stiff precision. Above him he heard the babylike shriek of a sparrow hawk. All around he felt the desert, pulsating and alive. Then there was the drumming of the calico's hooves and J.P. sat up again.

"It's all right," Cornflower said. "They were hunting antelope. I told them it was me they saw."

"They believed you?"

"Some did, but maybe not all. Chiricahua men are curious. They will argue awhile and maybe come back to see. I think we should leave this place."

They rode off the hill, although not side by side. Bravo refused to walk closer than ten feet to the Indian pony. Natanah led J.P. in the direction of the fort. Suddenly the Indian boy held up his hand.

From somewhere beyond a clump of greasewood trees came the sound of female voices. J.P. dismounted and joined Natanah, who was now on foot. They crept into the greasewood. Beyond the slick orange-red branches they saw Apache women with baskets. The women were on their knees as if searching for something lost.

"They're gathering mesquite roots for food," Natanah whispered. "The tall lady with the beads on her neck"—his voice was suddenly soft—"she is Summer Star, my mother."

"She's pretty," J.P. said.

"For a woman." He grinned. "Aren't you glad you weren't born a girl?"

"Very glad!" J.P. whispered it with much feeling.

"Women and girls frighten easily. Watch, I'll show you."

Before J.P. could answer, Natanah shook the greasewood branches and let loose a bloodcurdling yell. He was supposed to be a mountain lion. Then he stood with a grin and waited for the women to run.

But he didn't wait long. With loud yells the women picked up stones and hurled them at the greasewood branches. A dozen stones hit at the same time. One struck Natanah on the head, making him yell with pain. Others hit J.P., and each one hurt. Bravo took a stone on the end of his nose. His rusty yell of pain resulted in another shower of rocks.

The two boys had had enough. Quickly they mounted

and drove their animals away at top speed. This time even Bravo felt like running, at least for a short while.

"How easily they frightened," J.P. said sarcastically as he rubbed his sore head.

"I should have known better." Natanah grinned painfully. "My mother is afraid of nothing except evil spirits. That my father has found out many times."

Laughing, the two young friends continued in search of further adventures.

6

Arrested!

Shortly after noon Natanah showed J.P. the location of a food cache hidden beneath a three-armed saguaro cactus. The tree was marked with a tiny arrow cut in its trunk.

"In case our people are chased by soldiers," Natanah explained. "With hidden food a warrior can hide many days on the desert."

With his fingers he dug at the base of the ancient cactus tree and removed a rawhide packet. He and J.P. squatted in the shade of a rock and ate a quick meal of dried yucca flowers. J.P. had trouble swallowing the stuff. It tasted like burlap seasoned with glue.

"Good?" Natanah asked.

J.P. nodded. "Great."

If he could just keep from gagging . . .

Afterward the two boys sprawled happily on the ground. Both felt lazily comfortable. This spot was cool and completely hidden from the world.

"Tell me about the place where you live," Natanah said. "You know, the fort."

J.P. shrugged. "It's noisy and crowded with wagons and soldiers."

He told Natanah about Winchester Long and the Sioux talk. They laughed uproariously. "But if I had my way, I'd live somewhere else," J.P. added.

"Where?"

"Out here, I suppose."

Natanah nodded quick agreement. "You will when you're a scout."

J.P. looked away. There was a good chance now he'd never become a scout.

"Are you afraid of the dark?" Natanah asked suddenly.

"Sometimes."

"Apache boys are always afraid of darkness." He frowned. "There are so many things hard to understand, Ish-kay-nay. For instance, you know the band of light across the sky on summer nights?"

"Yes. We call it the Milky Way."

"So? Apaches believe it was caused by a horse who tripped while carrying a barrel of flour. What he spilled makes the light in the sky. Something else, Ish-kay-nay.

Have you ever felt and heard the earth tremble?"

J.P. nodded. "That's an earthquake."

"Ah. But to us it is the earth crying because of an approaching great sickness. Then there are stars that rush across the sky."

Meteors, of course. "What do they mean to you, Natanah?"

"They point the way at an advancing enemy."

Natanah told him of other Apache superstitions: a sneeze meant someone was thinking about you; ringing ears came from being talked about; watching a colorful sunset could cause sickness; and how warts were punishment for pointing toward Heaven with any finger other than the thumb.

"And bowlegs," Natanah said. "You know what causes bowlegs?"

J.P. said he had no idea, and he didn't.

"Eating frogs."

J.P. pointed at Bravo's legs. "He must have eaten a bushel."

Bravo knew when he was being talked about. He rolled his eyes insultingly and Natanah shook his head. "Maybe that one wouldn't even make a good meal."

Two healthy boys could only talk for so long, then they had to play. J.P. showed his friend the game of hopscotch. Cornflower in turn showed a marble game played with two round pebbles. J.P. won two games; Natanah won three.

Then they played tag–Apache style, and follow-the-leader–American style. Natanah led J.P. to a cottonwood tree and urged him to chew its small gray buds. J.P. found them to be somewhat like chewing gum, although not as tasty.

Finally they crossed a low hill and in the distance saw the smudged outline of Fort Bowie.

"There are horses there," Natanah said, and his eyes suddenly gleamed. "I learned to steal while I was still small. The old women hung deer meat strips in the sun to dry, and we little boys sneaked through the grass and stole the meat without being seen. Now I can steal a horse the same way."

J.P. was impressed. "Have you stolen any yet?"

"Two." Natanah's smile showed ivory-bright teeth. "Would you like to watch me steal a horse, Ish-kay-nay?"

J.P. said he could think of nothing he'd like better.

"Then I'll do it now. I'll get a horse from there."

J.P. was startled. Natanah pointed toward the civilian corral outside the walls of Fort Bowie. The very corral, in fact, in which Bravo spent his nights.

"That's a long way off," J.P. said uncomfortably.

"Maybe half a mile."

"And there are soldiers."

"Not outside the fort." Natanah was confident. "Follow me, Ish-kay-nay. We'll ride closer. Then I'll bring *you* a present."

J.P. wondered if he should argue. After all, those horses belonged to his neighbors. Yet he very much wanted to watch Natanah steal one in broad daylight.

They rode closer to the fort. Suddenly with a quick wave of his hand Natanah heeled his pony and galloped across the flat land toward the corral. Finally the calico pony stopped. Natanah leaped off its back and J.P. saw him tie it to a bush and disappear.

The white boy peered toward the community corral. He counted eight or nine horses inside that split-rail fence. J.P.'s eyes were very keen, but search as he might he could not locate the Apache boy. He stared so hard that after a while his eyes watered. But still he saw nothing. Was Natanah playing a trick on him? Maybe the Indian was lying somewhere on the ground, not even moving. Perhaps soon he would jump up with a wild laugh. . . .

Then the corral gate opened slowly. Was it possible? Still not the slightest sign of Natanah himself and yet—yes, a coal-black horse was moving toward the open gate. Now it was walking skitterishly through to the outside. . . .

J.P. knew that horse. It was a mare owned by a trapper named Christensen. Suddenly the mare started to gallop. Then, as if appearing from nowhere, Natanah was on the horse's back. Clouds of dust billowed behind them as the mare ran with long mane flying.

Natanah stopped to retrieve his pony, then rode up to J.P. Grinning, he leaped to the ground.

"You saw, Ish-kay-nay?"

"I saw." J.P.'s voice was thick with admiration. He climbed off Bravo's back. "But I can hardly believe it. Why, I never once saw you. Not even inside the corral."

Natanah laughed with pleasure. "My father says one must move like a spirit."

"You moved like a spirit, all right. A real skinny one." J.P. hesitated. "Now . . ."

"Yes, Ish-kay-nay?"

"Guess I'd better take the mare back. If someone sees me I can say she jumped the fence."

Natanah was puzzled. "Take her back? But why? I stole her for you, my friend. Now you can get rid of that cowardly burro."

Bravo snorted angrily.

"Afraid not, Natanah."

"I don't understand."

"I'd like to have her, of course." J.P.'s voice was wistful, the mare *was* a beautiful horse. "But her owner would know her by sight."

"I'll keep her for you," Natanah said. "Each time we meet, I'll bring her out for you to ride."

"I don't think so, Natanah."

The Apache's voice became stiff. "You will not accept my gift?"

"It isn't that. You know I'd love to have her. Except that . . ." J.P. was desperate; how could he explain without hurting his friend's feelings? "It's just that . . ."

Suddenly he had a new idea. "Natanah, didn't you say Apaches never steal from each other?"

"True."

"Well, some white men are the same way. To keep this man's horse would be stealing from him."

Natanah thought about it and finally nodded. "But you were proud of how I stole?"

"Very proud," J.P. said strongly.

"All right, Ish-kay-nay. You can take her back and I won't care."

J.P. took the rope. Suddenly the Indian boy stared over his friend's shoulder.

"*Soldiers come!*" he said in a strangled voice. "We run, Ish-kay-nay. Quickly!"

Natanah leaped into his pony's saddle, wheeled it around, and with pounding hooves rushed away. J.P. stood holding the rawhide rope that tethered the black mare. There was nothing else he could do. He heard the sounds of many hooves and the familiar rattle of sabers and spurs.

"Halt!" ordered a loud voice. Four troopers ringed J.P., Bravo, and the mare.

"Over there, sir. It's a Chiricahau, all right."

"You and Brooks go get him," snapped a young lieutenant with a cleanly shaven face and very long nose. The lieutenant—his name was Carlyle Simper, and he was the Colonel's adjutant—stared at J.P. peculiarly.

"You're the O'Flynn boy," he said.

J.P. nodded miserably.

"You're in bad trouble, fellow."

"For sure," muttered J.P.

He heard the squeaking wheels of Mrs. Blunt's approaching surrey.

"Whoa," she called out, and at the sight of Bravo her mouth trembled slightly. "What have we here, Lieutenant?"

"You know the lad, ma'am?"

"Certainly. Mrs. O'Flynn's boy, polite and very well brought up. But that filthy burro is something else again." Her eyes shifted. "Whose horse is that?"

The adjutant rubbed his nose. "I'd say she'd been stolen from the corral, ma'am."

"Stolen? By whom?"

Lieutenant Simper jabbed his thumb toward J.P. "Probably by him."

"Nonsense!" Mrs. Blunt snorted and leaned toward J.P. "You're not a thief, young man. You're the son of an honest scout and a fine woman. Tell this man you didn't steal that animal."

J.P. looked at the lieutenant. "I didn't, sir."

"It was either him or the Apache," declared the lieutenant.

Mrs. Blunt swung around, her eyes suddenly wide. "The *what?*"

"Apache. This boy was with an Indian. Two of my men are chasing him right now."

She licked her lips nervously. "Come closer, young man."

J.P. moved to the surrey.

"Is it true? Were you out here with an Apache savage?"

"With an Apache *boy*, ma'am."

"How old a boy?"

"Twelve, ma'am—and my friend."

She swung her head toward the lieutenant. "There!" she said triumphantly. "Hear that? Just a twelve-year-old Indian boy. Surely nothing for us to fear."

"Maybe not, Mrs. Blunt." The lieutenant smiled, and J.P. could see he and the lady weren't friends. "But you know your husband's orders. Apaches, and those who have dealings with them, are to be arrested on sight. And he didn't say adults only."

She sniffed loudly, but when she looked down at J.P. he knew she was worried. "I'm afraid that's the rule," she whispered.

J.P. nodded miserably. Maybe he'd be shot at sunrise. And when they brought in poor Natanah. . . .

But the two troopers returned without the Indian boy.

"Sorry, sir," said one, breathing hard. "Didn't even get close to him. His pony's too fast, and he knows the desert too well."

"What did he look like?"

"Well, sir—I'd say more like a boy than a brave."

"No matter. We'll return immediately and let Colonel Blunt decide what to do. Sergeant, place them under arrest."

The sergeant frowned. "The donkey too, sir?"

Mrs. Blunt laughed, and the adjutant flushed at his mistake. But the sergeant was one who obeyed orders. He wheeled his horse next to Bravo and J.P. "Prisoners–forward!"

Bravo began walking with ears flat against his head, looking sad and yet somehow angry, as if he'd known all along that darn Apache kid would get them into trouble. The Colonel's wife followed in her surrey, her mouth tight with anger. Her face showed determination to help the boy if she could.

And J.P.? Well, he was plenty worried, but there was also something for him to be glad about. At least Natanah had escaped.

7

Last Night at Fort Bowie

Colonel Hiram Blunt had commanded Fort Bowie for eighteen months. Never before had he been faced by a situation like this—horse stealing by a twelve-year-old boy!

His office seemed very crowded. There was the sergeant standing guard at the door, a big man in a blue uniform. Then Mrs. Blunt, who sat by her husband's desk and was getting ready to knit from a hank of wool she had taken from a bottom drawer. The Colonel paced slowly up and down, hands clasped behind his back, a ferocious frown twisting his face. He knew there was talk around the fort that his wife ran the post instead of him. The ferocious look was to make people think he was the boss.

At stiff attention close by stood Lieutenant Carlyle Simper. And there was J.P., of course, seated opposite the Colonel's wife. In the room filled with adults he looked terribly small.

Mrs. Blunt's knitting needles began to click. Colonel Blunt smiled at her. "My dear, I believe it best if you leave the room."

"I'm staying," she said without looking up.

"My dear, this is an official military investigation. . . ."

Her needles clicked. The Colonel glanced toward the door, but the sergeant was staring hard at the opposite wall. Then he looked at his adjutant, who frowned down at the floor. Colonel Blunt moved closer to the desk.

"My dear," he said in a low voice. "I would like you to leave."

She shook her head stubbornly. "Ordinarily I would, Hiram. But this is just a small boy, and I happen to like him. I'm going to stay and make sure that no one browbeats him."

J.P. had been taken to the Colonel's office without a single stop along the way. The Colonel turned to him suddenly and fiercely.

"Well, now!" the commanding officer said. "So you're a horse thief!"

Mrs. Blunt looked up from her knitting. "Not so loud, Hiram."

"Sorry, my dear." Then he saw the adjutant watching him and he said again, "A horse thief!"

J.P. looked at the picture of President Andrew Johnson high on the wall and didn't answer. It hadn't sounded like a question anyway.

"Yes or no," said the Colonel. "Are you or are you not a horse thief?"

"Please, Hiram. Not so loud."

"Sorry, my dear." He cleared his throat and in a softer voice said, "What's your answer, boy?"

"No, sir," J.P. said.

"No, sir, *what?*"

"No, sir, Colonel."

"No, sir, Colonel *what?*"

J.P. shrugged. "No, sir, Colonel. I'm not a horse thief."

"Humph!" breathed the adjutant.

Mrs. Blunt glanced at him sharply, and the adjutant flushed.

"How about it, boy?" said the Colonel.

"How about what, sir?"

"The horse."

"What about the horse?"

The Colonel blinked. "That's what I asked. How about the horse?"

J.P. was confused. "If you'd just ask what you want to know . . ."

"The Colonel asked if you stole the horse," said the young adjutant impatiently.

"No, sir, I didn't."

"I knew it," smiled Mrs. Blunt. "Hiram, this is just foolishness. You'd best let that lad go."

The adjutant shook his head. He wasn't really mean, but this was a good chance to make an impression on his commanding officer. "Sir, if I might ask him a few questions . . ."

The Colonel glanced at his wife. He certainly did not want to displease her. But there was that sergeant by the door and the lieutenant, both watching. . . .

"Go ahead," he said.

The adjutant stepped closer to J.P. "Young man, when we found you, were you or were you not holding a rope?"

"I was."

"And was the rope not tied to a horse?"

"Yes."

"Your horse?"

"No."

"Whose horse?"

"Mr. Christensen's horse."

The lieutenant flung a look of triumph at the others and stepped away. Colonel Blunt cleared his throat.

"So you stole Mr. Christensen's horse," he said quietly to J.P.

"No, sir."

The Colonel stared. "But you just said you *did*."

"No, sir. I said I was holding a rope tied to Mr. Christensen's horse."

The young adjutant became so excited that he pushed

the Colonel out of the way. "Wait a minute, boy. You mean that horse—excuse me, Colonel, sir—walked out to you from the corral because it *wanted to?*"

Mrs. Blunt looked up. "Foolishness!"

"I agree," snapped the Colonel.

"Then you stole that horse," the adjutant, now red-faced, said to J.P.

"Nope."

"Then who did?"

"Natanah did."

The Colonel blinked. Suddenly the adjutant remembered he'd forgotten to tell the Colonel the full story of J.P.'s capture.

"Sir," he said in a low voice. "The boy wasn't alone."

Colonel Blunt glared. "What do you mean?"

"Something—and someone was with him."

"What? Who?"

"A mangy-looking burro. And an Apache."

Colonel Blunt's gray hair seemed to stand on end. For months he had been fighting a losing war with the Apaches. He considered each of them more dangerous than a duffel bag loaded with rattlesnakes.

"But just a small Apache," Mrs. Blunt said quickly. "A mere boy."

"But one old enough to hold a rifle," insisted the adjutant.

She sniffed. "Don't be an idiot, Lieutenant."

"I'm trying not to be, ma'am. But please remember—"

"Silence!" insisted the Colonel. "Now listen to me, both of you . . ."

A green spider was spinning a web in the corner. Watching it, J.P. barely heard their argument. If their voices didn't bother the spider, he decided they shouldn't bother him either. After a while their voices calmed down. The Colonel looked at J.P. unhappily. "We're not getting anywhere, boy." He glared at the lieutenant. "I wish you hadn't even brought him here. But now I've got to finish this business."

The lieutenant's eyes widened and he snapped his fingers. "I just thought of a way he might help us, sir."

"Help us?"

"Yes, sir. For years we've been trying to capture Cochise. If we can get him, the rest of the Chiricahuas will probably surrender. That's where this boy can help."

"How? Hurry up . . . speak out!"

"We'll set a trap for Cochise and use the boy for bait."

"Bait?"

"Yes, sir." Lieutenant Simper's face shone, he was very happy with his idea. "We'll send him out to meet his red-skinned friend. The boy here will ask the savage to take him to the Apache camp. In the meantime we'll have two of our best scouts follow them. Once the location is learned we'll attack in strength."

"Hmm, it just might work." The Colonel nodded. "Good idea, Simper."

"Except for one thing," said J.P.

They all looked at him.

"I won't do it," he said in a small voice.

"Of course not," said Mrs. Blunt.

That caused the two men to argue again. Suddenly someone rattled the doorknob from the outside. Then there was a knock, and the sergeant looked at Colonel Blunt, who nodded, and the big soldier opened the door.

It was Mamacita.

"Juanito! What are they doing to you?"

"Nothing much, Mamá."

Her angry eyes flashed like hot coals as she glared at the Colonel. "Shame on you, Señor Colonel. Such a small boy . . ."

He swallowed timidly. "My dear lady–"

"Quiet!"

The young lieutenant blinked. "Now look, madam–"

"You, too–quiet!"

The Colonel's wife nodded with satisfaction. "I told them they were making fools of themselves, Mrs. O'Flynn."

"One moment," said the adjutant. "Madam, your boy has been associating with Apaches."

"I know who he's been associating with."

"But I said *Apaches*–"

"That is his business and mine, not yours."

"But–"

"He is my son, señor. A good boy, a proud boy, not someone to be questioned like a criminal. You understand that too, Señor Colonel?"

"I . . . yes, of course." Colonel Blunt nodded.

"All right, Juanito. Now we will leave."

With great dignity she walked from the room. J.P. followed, wondering if he should be embarrassed that his mother had come to help him.

In the room behind him he heard the Colonel say, "You young idiot! Why did you bother me with such foolishness?"

"Sorry, sir," replied the unhappy voice of the young lieutenant.

J.P. and his mother walked toward the main gate. The boy suddenly realized that something was wrong. The soldiers looked at him strangely as he passed, as if they were angry or even afraid of him. Word had probably gotten around. So this was how it felt to be known as the friend of an Apache—as if they thought he was their enemy. J.P. felt very sad.

Inside the adobe hut his mother ordered the smaller children into the back room; then, in a quiet voice, she said, "All right, Juanito. Tell me everything."

When he had finished she sighed and gazed sadly at the floor. "It is my fault."

"Why, Mamá?"

"My fault that you have grown up half-wild. We have done too much traveling, Juanito. We prospected for gold and hunted for furs. Now we live here near the Army post. This is no place for a growing boy. There are no schools, no boys your own age to play with. That is why you had to find a playmate out on the desert."

She touched his arm gently. "Juanito, I am going to send you to Tucson."

J.P. did not reply.

"My brother, Perez Mendoza, is a rich merchant in Tucson," his mother continued. "He will see that you are brought up as a young gentleman. You understand, Juanito? Right now there is much hard feeling about you at the fort. These people are terribly afraid of the Apaches. That makes them also afraid of an Apache's friend, even of a fine boy like yourself."

J.P. nodded. "Will you and Pepe and Maria go too?"

"Later, Juanito. After I know for sure what has happened to Papa. Then we will join you in Tucson. And, Juanito"—she took his arm and drew him very close to her—"remember that these people do not understand the ways of a boy like you. But we who are your family understand and love you very much . . ."

"Mamá," J.P. said in a small voice, "when I go, what will happen to Bravo?"

She looked away. "I am sorry, Juanito. The burro will have to stay in the corral with the other animals. Later perhaps I can sell him to someone who will be kind to him. You understand there is no other way?"

"Yes."

She watched a moment to see if he would cry. When he didn't she said, "Thank you, Juanito."

Later that evening Firechin Tom came to visit. When he heard about what happened, he agreed to take J.P. to Tucson on the stage. The boy should be ready to board at 5 P.M. tomorrow; the trip to Tucson would be run mostly after dark to avoid the Indians. Of course, said Firechin Tom, there would be no fare for the son of his old friend, Donegal Dan.

That evening while Mamacita was preparing Pepe and Maria for bed by the light of the coal-oil lantern, J.P. stole outside and walked unhappily to the corral. Somewhere in the darkness he heard a coyote howl.

How badly he would miss them all! There was no telling how long he would have to wait before Mamá and the children came to Tucson. With a wrenching of his heart J.P. suddenly knew that if his mother came to Tucson, it would mean his father was really dead. . . .

In the darkness Bravo nuzzled him with a wet nose. J.P. could no longer keep from crying. All right, now he knew what he'd do. He'd run away. This very night he'd go out there into the desert. His father was probably dead. His mother didn't love him or else why would she send him away . . . ?

"Juanito . . ." His mother was standing by his side, a small shadow in the darkness. "It's all right, my son. All right to cry. Because Mamá loves you very much . . ." She held him tightly. "And soon, after I know what happened to your father, I will be with you. You understand, Juanito? You understand how much you are loved?"

J.P. looked up at the stars that burned like white sparks in the great black desert overhead. Again he prayed that his father was alive.

Mamacita took his hand. "Let's go back."

Just before he turned away, J.P. saw a column of fire far out on the desert. An Apache fire signal. He didn't know its meaning so he made one up:

Do not worry, Ish-kay-nay. We will meet again someday. . . .

And suddenly he believed the imaginary message. "All right, Mamá," he said and smiled. "I'll do whatever you think best."

Arm in arm they walked back to the hut.

8

Rough Ride to Tucson

The moment had come. A red-and-yellow stagecoach stood almost loaded. Fading sunlight glinted against the gold letters "U.S.A." above the door panel. Firechin Tom and his shotgun rider, a tall thin man named Whiphandle Jones, carefully checked the harnesses on the four impatient horses.

Most of the passengers were already inside. J.P. O'Flynn leaned against the high rear wheel while Mamacita gave him last-minute instructions. Close by, Maria and Pepe sadly waited to say good-bye to their older brother.

"And the letter, Juanito. You have the letter to your uncle?"

"Pinned inside my shirt."

"Fine. He'll be surprised but happy to see you. Now then, Juanito . . ."

She talked rapidly about things he must be sure to remember. Like washing behind his ears and saying his prayers. How he should not get his feet wet. And how he must always avoid fighting with other boys. And most important of all, he had to remember always to act politely toward his uncle and aunt.

"You'll remember all this, Juanito?"

"I'll try," J.P. shuffled his feet with embarrassment. The other passengers were listening.

"Now kiss me good-bye."

Surely he was too grown up to kiss his mother. Especially while those people were watching. But he kissed her anyway, and it felt right, so he stopped worrying. Maria got a warm hug, Pepe a gentle rub on the head.

"You're the man now," J.P. told his little brother fondly. "Take good care of things."

"You bet." Pepe squared his narrow shoulders. "That means I can ride Bravo."

"Sure." But the thought made J.P. somewhat unhappy.

"I was going to fix sandwiches," Mamacita said. "But Tom says there'll be something to eat at the next stage station."

J.P. nodded. This was one time when he wasn't even hungry.

He didn't trust himself to speak. He climbed up the

hanging metal steps into the coach. Four people were sitting on the seats facing each other, and he sat between two men. He sneaked a quick look out the open door. Mamacita and the children were gone. He almost felt like running after them.

But beneath his sadness there was a small excitement. Not that he expected to enjoy himself in Tucson. It was just that traveling a hundred miles through Indian country was certainly an unusual adventure.

He nodded at the middle-aged lady sitting opposite him, and she nodded back without smiling. He wondered if she was as nervous as she seemed. Beneath a pink bonnet she wore her graying hair in a bun, and when she reached back to pat the bun, J.P. saw an enormous ring gleaming on her finger. At the end of her seat sat a fat man with a gleaming bald head who snored gently.

Firechin Tom climbed through the open doorway. "Everything all right, folks?"

J.P. nodded. The man on his left wanted to be sure his baggage was properly loaded. He said his name was Noah Muldoon; he was a clothing drummer on his way to Tucson with the latest samples of Eastern fashions. He liked to be sure they'd arrive in one piece.

On the boy's right sat a thin young man wearing what were maybe the fanciest clothes this side of London—a sleek bowler hat, bright red tie, white silk shirt, pearl-gray waistcoat, and spats covering the tops of gleaming leather

shoes. Yet despite these glorious feathers the dude appeared to be an unhappy bird.

"I'd like to ask one question," he told Firechin Tom in a shaky voice.

Tom's eyes leaped over the man's clothing. "Go ahead."

"Will there be much dust?"

The driver blinked with surprise. "Beg your pardon?"

"I said, 'Will there be much dust?' "

"Plenty."

"Oh, dear. It's so hard to stay clean in this awful land." The unhappy young man crossed his legs and leaned against a corner of the coach to sulk. Firechin Tom's mouth dropped open. Then he looked at J.P. and shrugged. What the heck; on the coach route one met all kinds.

"You comfortable, ma'am?"

The woman with the diamond ring shook her head. "Not at all, young man. I've traveled this far from Kansas. But my last hundred miles will surely be the worst."

"How's that, ma'am?"

"Apaches," she whispered nervously.

"Yes, ma'am." Firechin Tom couldn't argue with that.

Her eyes grew large. "I hear that just yesterday they found someone at the fort who's blood brother to an Apache."

Tom turned his eyes toward the roof. "That right?"

"Yes! Imagine a white man being friendly with those fiends." She saw J.P. staring at her and smiled. "Forgive me, sonny. I'm just an old woman who talks too much. If I frightened you speaking that way I'm sorry."

Still staring at the roof, Tom said, "You get a description of that white blood brother, ma'am?"

"Of course."

"Well, now," he said, and his eyes dropped, his expression becoming stern. "Suppose you describe him for us."

She nodded. "Six feet six–a giant. With only one eye and hair growing halfway down his back. A wild man, they say."

"Hmm." Suddenly Firechin Tom was smiling. "Know anyone fits that description, J.P.?

"No, sir," replied the boy in a small voice.

"Nor do I. Think I'd forget about him, ma'am. Can't hardly believe what you hear at an Army post. Rumors start and first thing you know they're exaggerated all out of shape."

"Something else I heard," she said breathlessly.

"Ma'am?"

"A rumor that this stage is carrying gold for the Army payroll. That there's a chance we'll be held up."

Firechin Tom shook his head. "See what I mean? You can't believe anything you hear. Now I'll try to set your mind at rest, ma'am. In case there's trouble, my shotgun rider is plenty experienced. If the Apaches or holdup men do come, they'll at least know they've been in a fight."

He winked broadly at J.P. and backed out the door. The

boy felt his heart slow to a regular beat. It would have been terrible for her to know the identity of the Apache's friend.

"O'Flynn," called a familiar voice from outside. "Say, there, O'Flynn."

J.P. jumped toward the window.

"For goodness' sake, be careful," complained the dude. "You're mussing my jacket."

"Sorry." J.P. grinned down at Big Bull Schultz.

"I just heard you were going, O'Flynn." The huge trooper frowned unhappily. "Too bad. Real bad, in fact. I feel awful for what happened. That dad-blamed old Colonel–"

"It wasn't his fault."

"Well anyway, I wish you a good trip. No matter what those folks say–you'll always be fine with me."

J.P. swallowed hard. "Thank you, Sergeant."

"And here's something to make your appetite happy. . . ."

He held up a tremendous chunk of dried beef, a loaf of bread and–more cream soda!

"Sergeant . . . thanks."

"Sure." Big Bull's teeth gleamed brightly. "Good luck, boy. I'm hoping to see you again real soon."

"Get ready to roll," Firechin Tom sang back at them. Feeling choked up, J.P. quickly returned to his seat. Mr. Muldoon, the clothing drummer, pulled out a small mouth organ and began blowing on it hard. Probably to keep from being scared, the boy guessed.

J.P. leaned against the leather seat and closed his eyes. Suddenly he was very sad. There had been no way to say good-bye to his friend Natanah. Nor to Bravo either . . .

"*Y-o-o-o team!*"

With a great rattle of wheels and chains, with the creak of springs and harness, the government stagecoach rolled toward the main gate and the vast desert beyond.

J.P.'s excitement about the adventure of a long stagecoach trip soon disappeared. It turned out to be the most uncomfortable situation he'd ever known. He was seated between Noah Muldoon and the fancy dude, whose name turned out to be Harrison Tulip. Both men had tug straps to grab. But seated in the middle, J.P. was at the mercy of every bump and chuckhole the wheels hit. The first time they struck an extra-deep hole, the boy was launched into the air as if from a slingshot. He landed squarely on the lady's lap. Face burning, he apologized. And a few minutes later he was on her lap again.

The lady—he thought of her only as "Mrs. Diamond Ring"—was naturally annoyed. But after a while she seemed to get used to his bouncing at her. Once she even tried to catch him in midair. Finally Mr. Muldoon stopped playing his mouth organ long enough to offer J.P. a coatsleeve to hold. That helped keep him in his seat.

Shortly before dark there was a brief stop while the shotgun guard lowered canvas curtains over the windows. That was so that if the men lit cigars, their matches wouldn't be seen by Indians outside.

The man on the seat with Mrs. Diamond Ring was still asleep and snoring. The shotgun guard paused to look down at him. Whiphandle Jones was the tallest man J.P. had ever seen. He also was the skinniest. About six feet, five inches tall—a fact that startled the lady when she first saw him—he couldn't have weighed more than 135 pounds. A floppy, dirty Stetson hung on his head, and his mouth moved constantly as a plug of tobacco slid from one side of his face to the other.

The passengers watched with interest as Whiphandle reached out to the sleeping man. Gently he pushed his chin upward until the man's mouth was closed. The snoring never stopped. Instead, it became louder.

"Beats all," muttered the tall man as he backed out the doorway. Mrs. Diamond Ring looked at the others and laughed, and a second later J.P. joined her. Laughing always made him feel better.

Again the stagecoach rattled on. Mr. Muldoon played softly on the small mouth organ, Harrison Tulip brushed himself time and again with a small whisk broom, and the fat man snored. In the deepening dusk the stagecoach became a small, noisy world. To J.P. it was more like a bouncing, jangling torture chamber. He clung desperately to Mr. Muldoon's sleeve. Once they hit an unusually deep hole, and he banged his head against the ceiling. When he looked at Mr. Muldoon, the man's eyes were popping and his mouth was stretched wider than a toad's. Frightened, J.P. slapped him hard on the back. The man finally spat out the harmonica he'd almost swallowed. After that Mr. Muldoon didn't play the mouth organ again during the entire trip.

It grew dark. Above the creaking and rattling J.P. heard the nervous breathing of Mrs. Diamond Ring, the monotonous snoring of the fat man, and the occasional *scratch-scratch* of Mr. Tulip's whisk broom. From his left came the deep breathing of Mr. Muldoon, who had somehow managed to fall asleep.

Four hours later the stagecoach stopped at the first stage station. By then J.P. was again thoroughly miserable. And he was more convinced than ever that being shipped to Tucson was about the worst thing that had ever happened to him.

9

A Dream Brings Trouble

"Just a quick stopover," Firechin Tom announced. "We've got to make miles before daylight."

J.P. dismounted with the others. Being younger he didn't groan as loudly. But he felt his muscles must hurt worse than theirs.

The stage station was just a few decrepit buildings surrounded by an adobe wall. In the yellow light of a five-day moon the passengers saw gaps where the wall was broken.

"Chiricahuas done that," one of the station hostlers said grimly. "We've been raided off and on for the last four months."

Mrs. Diamond Ring sighed nervously, and Mr. Muldoon whistled through his teeth. As the hostlers unharnessed the horses, Firechin Tom said cheerfully, "You'll find food inside, folks. Anything you want, so long as it's beef and beans. You'll also find a washing-up basin near the door. A special one for you, ma'am–with real soap. In thirty minutes we'll have a new team hitched. Then we'll be ready to roll."

This produced more groans. The passengers limped wearily toward the adobe buildings.

"Not hungry?" the driver asked J.P.

"I've got food. Be glad to share it, Tom."

"No thanks. Soon's we inspect the coach, Whiphandle and me are going inside for coffee."

The stationmaster brought a coal-oil lamp. By its light Firechin Tom and his shotgun rider checked the stagecoach. They examined the wheel hubs and axle ends, then Whiphandle crawled beneath and Tom handed him the lantern. A few seconds later the shotgun rider whistled loudly.

Firechin Tom winced. "That whistle means trouble," he said.

There was trouble all right. Two shackles were sheared clean through, a spring was badly ripped, and the rear axle was bent. No doubt the damage had been done by the same bump that had flung J.P. at the ceiling.

"Take a few hours to fix," Firechin Tom told his passengers a few minutes later inside the eating house. "Maybe till daybreak. We can decide then whether to run by day, or maybe stay here through tomorrow night."

Harrison Tulip shuddered. "You mean spend an entire night in this filthy place?"

"Afraid so."

Mrs. Diamond Ring's fingers fluttered to her throat. "Any danger of an Apache attack?"

"Always that danger," Firechin Tom admitted.

"Oh, dear . . ." Even in the dim lantern light her ring sparkled brightly. "After all these years I'd hate to lose my scalp."

J.P. shook his head. "Apaches hardly ever scalp, ma'am."

"The boy's right," Firechin Tom said. "Except now and then when they need a scalp for some medicine dance. If they raid here, they'll be after horses, not blood."

It turned out that, being only twenty miles from Fort Bowie, this stage station wasn't equipped for overnight visitors. The men agreed that the only woman in their party should have the eating house all to herself. They would find some place else to bunk.

J.P. picked the stable. There he found the hostlers still wiping down the team of horses that had brought them here. When they were finished and had gone, he made himself a hay pallet near the door, and almost immediately fell asleep.

As usual, he dreamed. This time, it was a dream about a strongbox filled with gold and a masked figure that robbed the stagecoach. Suddenly he was awake.

It took a few seconds to remember where he was. Then he heard snores all around him. He tried to count how many, finally guessed that at least six or seven men were sharing the stable with him.

In their stalls he heard the horses breathing fitfully. A wind blew in gusts, swinging the stable doors in and out on creaking hinges. Through the open doorway he saw the moon hanging low in the western sky. And he saw something else.

Near the stagecoach . . . a single indistinct figure. As J.P. watched, the figure reached upward toward the baggage bin. The bad dream was still strong in his mind. Almost the same scene as he was seeing right now. *Someone was stealing the gold.*

His first impulse was to yell. But that would only scare the robber away. Then J.P. would look very foolish. He thought hard and fast. So hard and fast that suddenly the Imp popped into his head.

Just one thing to do, it whispered. And J.P. did it.

Like a wild dog he bounded up from the hay and rushed out the door. Legs pumping furiously, he ran across the yard. With a wild shriek he hurled himself at the shadowy figure and gripped two very skinny legs.

The force of his rush knocked the figure over. The man dropped a shotgun. The shotgun went off with a roar like a giant thunderclap! Echoes rolled from the surrounding hills to disappear only slowly.

Behind him J.P. heard shouts, cusses, and one word repeated over and over:

"*Apaches! Apaches!*"

The men came pouring out of the stable. Inside the adobe house the frightened screeching of Mrs. Diamond Ring ripped the night like a saw blade cutting stone.

"Where are they?" someone yelled.

"Quick–to the walls!"

"Wait! Over *here*."

A lantern swung toward the ground. J.P. swallowed, looked up and smiled weakly.

"Howdy . . . er . . . folks."

"What happened?" asked Firechin Tom.

"I . . ." J.P.'s voice was scratchy and thin. "I guess I . . . made a mistake. . . ."

"Mistake!"

"Look over . . . er . . . there. . . ."

The lantern swung to one side. On the ground, shaking his head, sat Whiphandle Jones.

"Well, I'll be darned," breathed Firechin Tom. "You knock him down?"

"Afraid so, Tom."

"What do you know! Why, that's the first time I ever seen him dropped. What happened?"

"I thought he was a holdup man," J.P. explained miserably. "He was reaching toward the baggage bin and . . . well, I remembered talk about gold and all. . . ."

Whiphandle Jones suddenly spat a string of words that J.P. didn't understand. He figured it was just as well.

"I'll be darned," said Firechin Tom again. "I never heard him say so much at one time before."

Inside the eating house Mrs. Diamond Ring was still screaming. Rubbing his sore head, Whiphandle Jones squinted up at them. "Somebody keep her quiet," he said sourly. "And soon's I can stand I'm going to find out who knocked me down and . . ."

Firechin Tom grabbed J.P.'s arm. "Let's move, boy. He's working himself up to an awful meanness."

Together they hurried away to the stable.

"By the way," the stage driver said. "Where's that fat fellow? I didn't see him out there."

J.P. said he didn't know. He was too worried about Whiphandle Jones and his mean temper to care.

Inside the stable Firechin Tom hung the lantern on a nail and grinned. "By the way, J.P. There's no gold on the stage."

J.P. stared. "No gold?"

"Not this trip. Now you stay put while I try to calm Whiphandle down."

After the stage driver left, J.P. sat miserably on his pallet. This time he'd made an awful mess of things. No gold. Why, Mr. Jones was only standing Indian guard by the stage. That awful moment when he'd grabbed those skinny legs was one he'd never forget.

Suddenly he heard a strange sound. The horses? No. Horses didn't breathe that way.

He listened a while, then followed the sound to a hole in a big haystack.

"Excuse me," he called loudly into the hole.

"That you, son?"

It was a voice he'd never heard before. There was just one person it could belong to. "Are you . . . ?"

"Mr. Whipple, son. You probably never saw me awake. That's because I always sleep when I'm scared. Makes the time go faster."

There was the fat man from the stage. "What are you doing in there, Mr. Whipple?"

"Hiding."

"From what?"

"Apaches."

"Oh. Well, there are none."

"No Apaches?"

"None. It was a false alarm."

"Thanks."

J.P. waited for the man to come out, but he waited in vain. A few seconds later hearty, wet snores poured out from the haystack.

After a while the men tramped inside, talking about all that had happened. Then, one after another, they fell asleep. Soon J.P. began dozing too, but not before thinking how someday that gosh-darned Imp would get him into *real* trouble.

Right before dawn the stagecoach was again ready to roll. Firechin Tom had them vote on whether they wished to stay at the stage station until dark or take a chance on daylight traveling. The majority voted to travel.

One by one they climbed back into the coach. Firechin Tom said to J.P., "How'd you like to ride up in the driver's box?"

"Sure," the boy replied quickly. "But what about Mr. Jones?"

"Let's find out."

He lifted J.P. some six feet above the ground and into the driver's seat. Whiphandle Jones was already seated in his place with a mean-looking shotgun across his lap. He glanced at J.P., chewed slowly on his cud, and nodded.

"Howdy, boy."

Firechin Tom climbed up beside them and picked up the reins. "I don't think he's angry anymore," whispered J.P.

"Probably not," the driver whispered back. "He's decided to pretend last night never happened."

"How come?"

"Maybe so's he can forget a twelve-year-old kid knocked him down."

J.P. laughed. That made sense.

The ride to Tucson finally became an adventure for him. Traveling was still rough, but up on the driver's seat J.P. had things to grab. The great desert spread out all around them. Every twenty miles there were the mysteriously desolate stage stations waiting for their arrival. And always there was the breathless watch for an attack by Cochise. But it was an attack that never came. This was one trip on which the stage riders didn't even see an Apache. Or if they did, they didn't know it.

On the afternoon of the third day they passed the massive towers and white walls of the Mission San Xavier del Bac. The driver told him how the local Indians called this church the "White Dove of the Desert." Then nine miles later they saw Tucson.

"Well, there it is," said Firechin Tom, his red beard wagging happily. "What do you think?"

J.P. stared at what lay directly ahead. What did he think? Just this. That first chance he got, he was going to sure enough run away. Because Tucson was even worse than he'd imagined it could be.

10

First Week in Town

That first view of Tucson on a warm April morning in 1866 was one J.P. would never forget. First came the whitewashed walls rising above the flat landscape like a box-shaped hill. As they came closer he saw that against those walls sat some of the dreariest little shacks he could ever imagine existed.

They rolled through the gateway. He was hit by noise—the shrill sounds of shouting men, braying mules, barking dogs, and the rattle and screech of wagons. Firechin Tom slowed the stagecoach to a crawl. Carefully he guided the horses through strings of Army wagons, prairie schooners, and flat wagons loaded with hay. The streets themselves were narrow, without sidewalks and spotted with dried mud. The buildings looked half ruined, as if they had been through an Indian attack. Squawking chickens fluttered before the horses' legs. Now and then a wildly squealing pig ran between the buildings, followed by its owner in hot pursuit. To this boy from the desert, the world suddenly seemed a place of noise and terrible confusion.

"How do you like it?" asked Firechin Tom with a broad grin.

J.P. shook his head. "All this noise. And all those wagons . . ."

"Waiting their turn at the Quartermaster Depot. Remember, everyone for five hundred miles around sells his produce here to the Army."

In the town square before a partially built church, J.P. saw rows of prairie schooners with their inhabitants camped alongside. Right on the main street they were cooking over small wood fires.

J.P. shook his head again. "I–I don't think I like this place, Tom."

"No one does at first. But you'll get used to it."

Maybe he would. But right now J.P. just couldn't see how.

After long minutes of waiting, starting, and waiting again, they finally rolled up to the stage depot. Firechin Tom showed him the location of his uncle's establishment.

"Down that way, then cut right. It's a store with a new warehouse behind. Your uncle's name is on the sign."

When J.P. hesitated, the stage driver grinned understandingly. "Now don't get cold feet, J.P. Tucson isn't big as it looks. Just five hundred people, not counting the soldiers and overnight folks. Barely fifty of those are Americans."

"Will I see you again before you leave?"

"Not this trip. We're pulling out first thing in the morning. But I'll be back in about a week, so look for me then. I'm sure to have a message for you from Fort Bowie."

Mrs. Diamong Ring shook hands with J.P. Then he said good-bye to Mr. Muldoon, who could still barely speak, and to Mr. Harrison Tulip, who seemed on the verge of a dusty nervous breakdown. There was a brief nod from Whiphandle Jones. Mr. Whipple still looked sleepy, but he shook hands with J.P. in a lively way. Then the boy turned and walked through the bedlam that was Tucson, boom town of the Arizona Territory.

He got as far as the half-built church when a loud yell brought him up short.

"*Stop, you scalawag!* Not another step!"

J.P. froze. The shouts came from a very angry farmer sitting on the front seat of a covered wagon.

"Hear me? I said *stop!*"

"I *am* stopped," replied an annoyed J.P. Then he realized the farmer wasn't yelling at him at all, but at a tall boy standing near a pile of adobe bricks in front of the half-built church. The boy held a brick under one arm.

"Drop it!" yelled the farmer.

The boy made a nasty face at the farmer and ran. The

man was so angry that he leaped off his wagon after the boy. The two mules hitched to the wagon were unattended, so J.P. held the reins until the man returned, puffing loudly.

"Well, now," he said gruffly. "At least there's one kid in this town with manners. Thanks, son."

The man's neck was raw and sunburned, as if he had driven the wagon all day in a hot sun. "Excuse me," J.P. said, "but what did he do?"

"Do?"

"That you should yell at him and chase him, I mean."

"He was stealing bricks, that's what." The farmer pointed at the cluttered pile of adobe bricks. "They're kind of hard to come by out here. And I hate stealing."

The farmer wiped his face with a bright-red bandanna. "If I wasn't selling my corn to the Army, I wouldn't come near this town. But that's my worry and not yours. See you around, boy."

He giddapped the mules, and J.P. continued walking until he reached a small store in front of a busy warehouse. A sign above the store read, PEREZ MENDOZA, GENERAL MERCHANDISE. J.P. felt for Mamacita's letter pinned inside his shirt. His heart was beating fast. He took a deep breath and walked inside.

He saw shelves loaded with cans and bottles and cheeses and meats hanging from the rafters by strings. Food smells tickled his nose, and on the shelves sat things so mysterious that he couldn't even guess what they were. There was a thin woman with a kindly face who smiled and said, "Can I help you, young señor?"

J.P. tried to say hello but couldn't find the words. He nodded, reached inside his shirt and pulled hard. The pin ripped his shirt. The sound startled the woman, but suddenly her face lit up.

"Wait," she said softly. "Your face . . . are you Juanito, my sister-in-law's boy?"

J.P. nodded.

"So . . ." For a long moment she just looked at him. Then gently she touched his shoulder. "Come, Juanito. Let us go find your Uncle Perez. He will be very happy to see you."

Suddenly he was flooded with warmth. Having her smile at him like that meant things were only half as bad as he thought they were.

Perez Mendoza turned out to be a heavily set man with thick black hair and sharp, dark eyes. That night he explained his business to his nephew.

"At first we had just the store," he said with a Spanish accent while he waved a long black cigar. "But for the last year, ever since the end of the war between the North and South"—he blew a heavy cloud of smoke—"the Army has tried to open the West. The Indians are fighting it, of course. Which means we need many forts, all of which must be supplied with food and merchandise. By very good luck Tucson was chosen as the central supply headquarters.

Quickly my store grew into a warehouse. You see, I buy from Mexican farmers and cattlemen and sell to the United States Army."

Then J.P. was told of his uncle's plans for him.

"You will work in the store." Uncle Perez smiled as if doing him a great favor. "Aunt Martha can then work with me in the warehouse."

Aunt Martha looked startled. Apparently his uncle had not talked it over with her in advance. "I'll teach you the prices," Perez Mendoza continued. "Then you can handle what little business there is in our store."

Being a store clerk didn't really appeal to J.P. But it seemed he had no choice. . . .

"And school?" he managed to ask.

His uncle frowned. "School?"

"Mamá said you'd want to send me to school."

"Someday," replied Uncle Perez after an embarrassed cough. "But not yet. Not only because I need you in the store, but also because we don't yet have a school in Tucson. I am sure you will be happy working for me."

"Maybe," J.P. replied dubiously. "Only I wonder what my father would think of me clerking store."

"I'm sure he would be displeased," Uncle Perez answered sharply. "Your father never saw anything good about settling down."

The harsh sound in his voice gave J.P. something to wonder about. Did Uncle Perez dislike his father?

The next morning Juanito Patrick Mendoza O'Flynn

became a store clerk. His mind was quick, and after just a little practice he learned most of the prices. Coal oil sold for $8.00 a gallon, sugar for 75¢ a pound. Coffee was $1.50 per pound, while a single bar of soap cost 50¢.

But just knowing the prices didn't make his work fun. In fact, J.P. found it downright boring. There were very few American customers, and those who spoke Spanish usually selected their own goods. J.P. could hardly understand them. Although Mamacita knew Spanish, of course, she never spoke it enough at home for him to learn.

One thing he sold in great amounts was bleached flour. It went for 18¢ a pound and was bought mostly by young Mexican women. J.P. finally realized that their pale-white complexions did not mean they were sick. It just meant they were using the flour for face powder!

At the end of his third day in Tucson he felt no better about things than he had on the first. In fact, his homesickness grew worse with each passing minute. On the fourth day he was pleased to see a familiar face enter the store. It was the dapper dude he had met on the stagecoach, Mr. Harrison Tulip. By now the man's fancy clothes seemed to have been worn a few days too many.

After the hellos, Mr. Tulip said that he'd come to purchase a new whisk broom. The other had simply worn away.

"It's this terrible town." The man sighed. "Probably the dirtiest, dustiest place in the whole world. I simply can't wait to leave."

"And when will that be, sir?"

"Unfortunately I don't know. I'm hoping to reach California someday. But I must wait until my sister sends money from San Francisco. Dear me, I hope she hurries. I'm down to my last change of socks."

"If you need a loan before your money comes, Mr. Tulip, I'll try to fix it with my uncle. Stuff like cigarette makings or food, why just help yourself and pay later."

For a moment Mr. Tulip was silent. Then in a voice that hardly sounded like his own, he said, "Thank you, young man. You're very kind." His voice changed back to its usual prissiness. "But I've enough money to last another week. That is, if this awful dust doesn't kill me first."

"Do you know what happened to Mr. Muldoon, sir?"

"He finally went on to Yuma. So did that woman and the sleepy fellow, although what they'll do in Yuma I can't imagine. I hear there's nothing there but soldiers."

J.P. said he didn't know. After sneezing a few times and complaining about the dust, Harrison Tulip picked up his new whisk broom and walked out.

Two days later J.P. was wiping the glass counter when someone coughed. He looked up and found himself looking into two familiar dark eyes.

"Howdy, boy."

"Mr. Long!" J.P. smiled. "What are *you* doing here?"

"Rode in with an Army mule train," said Winchester Q. Long. "Things got too slow for me back at Bowie. Figure a booming town like this holds more opportunities." He winked mischievously, and J.P. laughed. "How about yourself, boy?"

J.P. told him about his uncle and the store, and Winchester Long nodded. "I heard about your trouble at the fort, of course. The way folks worried about it, you'd think you was Cochise's grandson. By the way, I came in for a sack of Bull Durham."

J.P. removed a sack of tobacco from a glass jar and took the coins the man held out. "Hope I'll be seeing you around, sir."

"You might." Suddenly there was a funny look on Mr. Long's face. "That is, if you want to know me after today."

"What do you mean?"

"Could be I done too much talking since coming to Tucson."

J.P. didn't understand. "Talking?"

"About you and your Apache friend. Sorry, boy, but I didn't know you was in town. Seemed a good story to tell in the cantinas while waiting for a poker game. Trouble is, folks in Tucson hate Apaches even worse than they do in Bowie."

J.P. became worried. He didn't want his uncle's business getting hurt because of him. But that's exactly what happened. The next day business slowly dwindled. By late afternoon hardly two people had come into the store. Uncle Perez frowned when he counted the day's receipts.

"Business is very bad, Juanito."

"I know, sir."

"However, I don't think we should mention it to your aunt. Today is her birthday. I see no reason to spoil that with bad news. You agree?"

J.P. said he did.

"But Juanito . . ." His uncle frowned again. "Do you know any reason why business is so bad?"

J.P. knew his uncle couldn't help but blame him. Maybe he thought he was stealing the profits. "I think I do, sir."

"Yes, Juanito?"

"It's my fault . . ."

He felt utterly miserable. His uncle watched him a while; then his expression softened. "Don't be afraid, Juanito. Just tell me everything."

J.P. told him—about Natanah, about what happened at Fort Bowie, and about Winchester Long's recent visit.

"I see." Uncle Perez had a peculiar light in his eyes. "Wait here, Juanito. I will go see if people have really turned against us."

Uncle Perez was only gone a few minutes.

"It is very serious," he said. "Rumors have spread that my nephew is a friend of the Apaches. I'm sorry, Juanito. But many people have little to do, and they enjoy bad rumors. And everyone is afraid of the Apaches."

"What are they saying, Uncle?"

"It does not matter."

"Please tell me."

"Well . . ." Uncle Perez shrugged. "They say the

profits made in our store will be used to buy guns for the Indians."

"A lie!" cried J.P. desperately. "What can we do?"

"I'm not sure." Uncle Perez smiled wanly. "We'll think about it a while. Meantime I think we can close the store early. Would you like the afternoon off?"

J.P. said it didn't make much difference to him. Then he decided that anything was better than standing behind that counter waiting for customers who didn't come.

Walking through the noisy town, he wished he had at least one friend his own age. But here, as everywhere else, getting to meet kids was difficult.

At the Quartermaster loading dock he watched wagons move slowly up to the wooden plaform. There was even some excitement when the soldiers arrested a farmer who was selling molasses, except that an alert lieutenant discovered some of the molasses barrels filled with creek water instead of sweet stuff.

A man standing next to J.P. told him this happened quite often. Lots of people tried to cheat the government, and too gosh-darned many were getting away with it. J.P. walked away shaking his head. What a place, he thought.

A few blocks farther on he saw a blindfolded burro walking around a circular path. It was hitched to a well handle. Each time the burro made a full turn, water poured into a large trough. The burro was too old and thin to look much like Bravo. But just seeing his four legs and long face brought an ache to J.P.'s heart.

"Hey, kid, you want a bucket of water?" asked a swarthy man sprawled on a wooden crate. "Just five cents a bucket."

"No, thanks."

The man scowled. "You don't want nothin'?"

"Nothing."

"Then get away."

J.P. obligingly walked away. A few blocks later he found himself crossing Whiskey Row, a short, dirty street lined with shabby cantinas. Through the slatted swinging doors he heard singing and laughing, but this wasn't a street for kids, so he picked up speed. Then, passing one door, he stopped because the voice he heard inside was familiar.

"A friendly game of poker, gentlemen. Just a little fun to pass away a slow, hot day."

It was the voice of Winchester Q. Long, gay and easy and sure of himself. Then J.P. heard another voice that he recognized as belonging to the red-necked farmer with the wagonload of corn.

"I'll play with you, mister. Haven't much cash, but I'll wager my wagon and corn against whatever you've got."

J.P. walked away feeling slightly sorry for the red-necked farmer. Somehow Winchester Long seemed a hard man to beat at anything.

After supper Uncle Perez put down his napkin and smiled fondly at Aunt Martha. "My dear," he said with a wink at J.P. "Of course you know that today's your birthday."

"My birthday? Goodness . . ." Her turn to wink at the boy. "Why, I'd forgotten all about it. Thank you for remembering, dear Perez."

"And I have a little present for you," said Uncle Perez with an excited smile. "If you'll please close your eyes, my dear . . ."

With her face flushed, and smiling, Aunt Martha closed her eyes. Quickly Uncle Perez removed something from his pocket. He held it up for J.P.'s approval. Then he lifted his wife's hand and slipped the gleaming bracelet over her wrist.

"Can I open my eyes now?" Aunt Martha asked.

"Yes, my dear. And a happy birthday to you."

She was so pleased with the bracelet that she hugged and kissed her husband. She showed it to J.P. at least three different times. He smiled and each time said it was beautiful.

"Where did you find such a beautiful bracelet, Perez?" Aunt Martha asked, her face still flushed with pleasure. "I didn't know there was a diamond to be had anywhere east of San Francisco."

"That's where it came from. I ordered it six months ago."

"Perez," she said with shining eyes. "Thank you very much, my dear."

After that Uncle Perez brought out a guitar and began

strumming it with nimble fingers. Aunt Martha showed J.P. how to do the Mexican hat dance, and while Uncle Perez's fingers flew across the strings, the boy and his aunt jumped wildly around an old sombrero on the floor. J.P. tripped over his own feet and fell, but he didn't hurt himself. He sat laughing while his aunt and uncle howled with glee.

After a while some neighbors joined the party. There was much to eat and drink. With the dancing and singing J.P. had such a gay time that he suddenly realized that he had almost forgotten about his family and Natanah. He was just beginning to feel guilty when his aunt grabbed his hand and pulled him to where the sombrero waited on the floor. There was much clapping of hands and loud singing.

They had so much fun that J.P. forgot his troubles all over again.

11

Wagons Filled with—What?

The morning after the birthday party he was awakened by the hoarse cry of the water peddler outside:

"*Water here! Five cents a pail! Who needs water today?*"

J.P. thought of places in the world where folks had all the free water they could use. The only time he had seen such a place was when they had gone prospecting in the Sierra Madre mountains. There they had found rushing streams and wide blue lakes. But here in Tucson water was so scarce that only women took baths at home. The men either used the public baths at *El Ojito*, "Little Eye Springs," or else did without.

"*Get your water, friends. Five cents a bucket and going fast . . .*"

J.P. got up from his rope-spring bed. He peered through the barred opening that served as a window. The water cart was two-wheeled and drawn by a—

Oh my gosh. He was hit by a pang of misery. That cart was drawn by a burro looking so much like Bravo that he almost bawled. Miserably he dropped back on the bed. Memories ran through his head, and each brought a solid

lump to his throat. Not only memories of his burro, but also of Mamacita, Pepe, Maria—and most of all, of poor Donegal Dan.

"Juanito?" Aunt Martha was in the doorway. "You feel all right?"

J.P. nodded, face turned away so she couldn't see his misery.

"Then you'd better dress," she said. "Uncle Perez thinks you and he should open the store this morning."

"You know it was my fault that business got bad?"

"I know about your Indian friend. But neither Perez nor I think you should feel any blame."

After breakfast he and Uncle Perez walked toward the store. "When will your friend with the stagecoach return, Juanito?"

"Any day, I guess. In fact he's overdue." He looked up at his uncle. "You suppose Cochise finally got Firechin Tom?"

Uncle Perez smiled. "From what I hear, your friend is more likely to get Cochise."

A stream of Army wagons lumbered by, forcing the man and boy to flatten themselves against a building. J.P. noticed wet places in the street where the water wagon had spilled over. While he stood looking at the spots—in Tucson wet mud was as rare as snow—a fat pig came squealing down the street. Its owner, even fatter than the pig, ran after it puffing loudly and yelling in a hoarse voice:

"Stop, you blithering porker! Stop, I say!"

The pig must have broken loose from a cattle wagon. That seemed to happen all the time. J.P. saw the animal coming fast. He judged the distance from himself to the pink porker and jumped for it. He missed and landed in a patch of thick mud.

The fat man tripped over him and so, instead of thanking the boy for trying, he was angry as he staggered up wet and dripping and continued on the run. Plastered with muck, J.P. shrugged up at his uncle.

Perez Mendoza laughed so hard that his eyes looked like black buttons wet with dew.

"I'm sorry," J.P. said as he stood up and tried to brush himself off. With these clothes he would hardly be able to work today.

"At least it was for a good cause." His uncle laughed. "Come on."

"Home?"

"Not like that. We'll go to the public baths at *El Ojito*. I'll see that you really get clean."

The public bathhouses at Little Eye Springs could be heard a long way off. That was because of the roaring boiler which heated the bath water. The bathhouses themselves were small wooden shacks located in the middle of a grove of tamarisk trees. A sign above a small ticket window read:

BATHS
Hot—25¢
Cold—15¢

Uncle Perez bought a ticket for J.P. and led him into a small shed. There in lonesome glory sat a discolored tin bathtub mounted on scrolled legs. The legs ended in giant claws clutching a metal ball. As J.P. and his uncle watched, an attendant brought two large buckets of steaming water and poured them into the tub. A moment later he returned with two buckets of cold water, a slightly dirty towel, and a bar of brown soap.

"Suggest you go easy on the soap," he said. "It's strong enough to peel off your hide."

"Give me your clothes," said Uncle Perez. "I'll dry them by the boiler. Then maybe the mud will rub off."

J.P. stripped and handed him his clothing. His uncle shut the door behind himself. In the gloomy interior of the shed J.P. climbed into the tub. At first the water felt too hot, but after a few moments it became stimulating and luxurious. This was the first good washing he'd had since leaving Fort Bowie.

From all directions he heard men's voices. The bathhouses were favorite places for talking business, telling jokes, or just plain old-fashioned gossiping. The chinks in the plank walls made it easy to talk back and forth.

Then, from another tub close by, he heard someone humming. A smile broke out on J.P.'s face.

"That you, Mr. Tulip?" he called.

The humming stopped. "Who's there?"

"J.P. O'Flynn."

"Hello, young man."

"I heard you humming, sir."

"Yes . . . I suppose I was."

"You sounded happy."

"Well, I'll tell you. Getting clean *is* happiness for me. But now I'm sad again."

"Oh. Sorry, sir."

"It isn't your fault. I just happened to remember that my money still hasn't come. Matter of fact, yesterday I had to sell my watch."

"That's too bad."

"Understand you have troubles too, young man. I heard the rumors."

"They aren't true," J.P. said hotly.

"Of course they aren't. But people around here probably can't help being mean. It's all this dust. Gets into the blood and clogs their thinking."

J.P. heard a loud sigh, and then Harrison Tulip said good-bye. J.P. could hear water slosh as the man left his tub.

After J.P. had slipped back into his clothes which his uncle had dried and returned to the shed, the two of them walked slowly back toward the store.

"Feel better, Juanito?"

"Much better, Uncle."

"Good. Nothing like cleanliness to lift a man's spirits. And be sure that from now on you watch out for pigs." Uncle Perez laughed again.

He looks nice when he laughs, thought J.P. Almost like Mamacita.

Business remained bad. J.P. spent one long hour after another just leaning on the counter. He watched spiders build webs, flies stroke their legs, and ants march stupidly across the wall in single file. An occasional mouse ran stealthily over the floor. The store seemed filled with everything except customers.

His unhappiness increased. Nothing was worse than having nothing to do. Right now he seemed to have more of nothing to do than did anyone else. After a while he began standing in the doorway of the store and watching people walk by. Now and then he sighed and wondered why he hadn't stayed at Fort Bowie. It couldn't have been much worse for him there.

Suddenly three wagons in a row, each pulled by two strong mules, came creaking down the street. The second and third wagons were each led by a rope from the lead wagon. The driver waved to him cheerfully.

It was Winchester Q. Long. And a completely changed Winchester Q. Long, at that. The would-be scout was no longer dressed in the familiar buckskin. Instead he wore a black frock coat, broadcloth trousers, and shining leather boots. Mr. Long looked very prosperous indeed.

J.P. watched the small wagon train move down the street. A riddle tickled his mind. Mr. Long had apparently won the farmer's wagonload of corn, but how the heck had he gotten *three* wagonloads?

J.P. thought about it in the silence of the store. The more he thought, the more interesting the problem seemed. Where had Mr. Long found all that corn? And how had he come by it?

Not that it was any of J.P.'s business. But right then he didn't have any other business. The wagons were headed for the Quartermaster dock. J.P. wondered if he should sneak away for a few minutes and look inside them.

Except who would mind the store? No one, he finally decided. He would just lock the door. And if Uncle Perez didn't like that, well he could just . . .

Send me back to Fort Bowie, thought J.P. defiantly.

He felt a small tingle of excitement. At last he had something to do. He padlocked the front door and hurried toward the Army freight dock.

12

The Imp Saves a Friend

There were the usual lines of wagons waiting their turns to unload at the Army warehouse. And the wagons were of all kinds. J.P. saw huge Conestogas with their boat-shaped beds. He saw two-wheeled Mexican oxcarts with seven-foot wheels, also prairie schooners, surplus Army freight wagons, and homemade contraptions of weird sizes and shapes. The mule skinners and bullwhackers sat perspiring in the hot sun, spitting tobacco juice and impatiently eyeing the prison crew that unloaded the wagons at the depot.

Winchester Long and his canvas-covered wagons sat far back on line. Mr. Long sat on the front seat of the first wagon, fanning his face with a black planter's hat. That gave J.P. a chance to sneak up to the end of his rear wagon. He avoided another runaway pig and waited until its owner had passed, yelling furiously. Then, gripping the wagon tailpiece, he boosted himself inside.

The cargo space was raised by sideboards. The heat felt ferocious, the sweet smell of hot corn almost sickening. Dropping to his hands and knees, he began digging through the short white ears, but not for long. Maybe a foot below the top he struck something that definitely was not corn. With a grin he kicked corn ears back into the hole he'd made and lowered himself outside to the ground.

So now he knew. Only what should he do about it?

While he stood thinking, another big porker came bounding along the dusty street. Just as J.P. was about to step out of its way, he felt a satisfying *thump*. The Imp was back inside his head.

It took some doing to catch that fast-moving pig. Finally he managed to grab it by one ear. The pig squealed as J.P. gripped it under the belly and heaved it high and into the wagon. A moment later two more pigs came bounding along. J.P. caught one, the other got away. The new captive also went into the wagon.

The owner of the pigs wore gold-rimmed glasses and a tremendously large hat. "You see my pigs?" he shouted.

"Yes, sir." The boy pointed. "One went that way."

The man took off in that direction. J.P. breathed a sigh of relief. He hadn't really lied—one *had* gone that way.

Now there was nothing to do but wait. And wait he did,

standing in a small patch of shade near the Army warehouse. He listened to the sounds of prison swampers, of the wagon owners arguing with the Army lieutenant over prices. He heard the braying of mules, the howling of drivers, and the mixed-up sounds of wheels, pigs, chickens, geese, and goodness knew what else from inside the wagons. Flies buzzed lazily in the heat, and J.P. felt sleepy. But finally he saw Mr. Long's wagons, now about sixth in line from the Quartermaster depot. J.P. walked out from the shade and approached the darkly clad figure.

"Hello, Mr. Long."

"Afternoon, boy."

J.P. grinned up at him. Finally Mr. Long said, "Want something, boy?"

"Nope." J.P.'s grin grew broader. "Nice wagons, sir."

"Thank you, boy. Won them in a friendly game of chance."

"All three?"

"Well, not exactly. One to be exact." He winked. "But a little natural business sense turned them into three."

The wagon in front of them rolled forward. Mr. Long giddapped his mules and then stopped them again. He was now five wagons from the loading dock.

"What you got inside them, sir?"

"Corn. Thirty bushels per wagon, about a thousand dollars' worth, all told."

"An awful lot of money."

"A fair amount." The long-haired man grinned. "About enough to help me start making more."

"And the pigs, sir? How much are they worth?"

Winchester Q. Long blinked. "Pigs?"

"Yes, sir."

"What pigs?"

"Those in your rear wagon."

Again the wagon in front moved forward. Mr. Long sat staring at J.P. until the lieutenant on the dock yelled for him to roll ahead. When he again stopped his mules, Mr. Long was four wagons from the depot. He put down the reins and leaned toward the boy. "You say something about pigs?"

"In the rear wagon, sir."

"Hmm." Dark eyes narrowed. "Let's go take a look."

He climbed down, and J.P. followed him to the back of the rear wagon. They grabbed hold of the tailpiece and pulled themselves up to the opening in the canvas top. Side by side J.P. and Winchester Q. Long stared inside.

The two pigs had rooted deeply into the stacks of corn ears. Sticking up through the holes they'd caused were the sharp edges of adobe bricks, the same bricks that J.P. had last seen before the unfinished church.

They stared for a long time; then Mr. Long looked at J.P. "Boy, how you suppose those bricks got in my wagon?"

"Hard to say."

"And those pigs. You ever heard of pigs climbing into a wagon?"

"No, sir."

They dropped back to the ground. Mr. Long looked very thoughtful.

"Guess you think my other wagons are salted with bricks too," he muttered.

"Guess I do, sir."

"And those soldiers might not take kindly to bricks passed as corn."

"No, sir. They might not."

Winchester Long suddenly brightened. "Of course, I might have planned talking to them when they examined my cargo. There's folks who say when I talk, why, I can make anyone believe almost anything. Maybe I planned they wouldn't examine my wagons too well."

"Maybe so."

His face clouded again. "Then again a man might get caught."

"Yes, sir, he might."

"Someone might even tell on him. . . ."

J.P. grinned. "Someone sure might."

"Hmm . . ." Winchester Long's eyes narrowed, and he thoughtfully stroked his moustaches. "Makes it hard for a fellow to decide what to do."

They heard the lieutenant yelling again. They hurried to the front wagon and again Mr. Long led the mules toward the wooden depot. Now he was just three wagons away.

"Mighty hard to figure," repeated Mr. Long.

"Sir . . ."

"Huh?"

"A suggestion," J.P. offered bashfully.

"What's that?"

"A man could put those bricks back after dark."

"Hmm." Winchester Long seemed to be in pain. Suddenly he climbed down from the driver's seat and strode toward the loading dock. J.P. followed at his heels. The Army lieutenant was perspiring in the hot sun. He stood watching as two swampers counted heads in a wagon loaded with sheep. Winchester Long looked up at the lieutenant. "Got time for a question, young man?"

The soldier nodded. "Go ahead."

"Just to settle our curiosity, sir. Is it true some folks try to short-count you?"

"True enough. We caught another one this morning."

"Despicable!"

"A man from California selling lemons. Two layers of fruit and the rest was sand."

Mr. Long looked shocked. "The scoundrel."

"But that's one trick that hardly ever gets by me." The lieutenant smiled. "You might say that finding 'salters' is my specialty."

The long-haired man licked his lips. "That so?"

"Yup. My first day on duty here I found a wagon salted with gravel. It kind of interested me in the subject." He grinned. "Matter of fact, I've found so many since that now my men call me 'Salty.' "

J.P. said, "What happens to those you catch, sir?"

"It's standard punishment, son. Ten years in jail."

Mr. Long drew in his breath. The lieutenant looked at him peculiarly and said, "Say, aren't those your wagons down there?"

"Er . . . wagons?"

"Better get ready to move them up. We'll be checking your load in a few minutes."

Mr. Long glanced sideways at J.P. and whispered, "Think I'll just be going, boy. See you around . . ."

The lieutenant stared at him suspiciously. "What's that you said, mister?"

"I . . . me?" He tried to smile. "Why, nothing . . ."

"He's worried about his wagons, sir," said J.P.

Mr. Long suddenly trembled.

"Worried?" asked the lieutenant.

"Yes, sir. They're loaded with bricks."

The boy grabbed Winchester Long's arm. Except for that, the long-haired man would have broken into a run.

"Bricks!" exclaimed the lieutenant.

"Yes, sir," said the boy. "Adobe bricks."

Winchester Long sighed. It sounded exactly like a moan to J.P.

The soldier looked from them to the three wagons, then slowly shook his head. "Sorry, mister. But the Army doesn't buy bricks. They're too heavy to transport. Guess you'd better pull your wagons out of line and let the fellow behind you move up."

Mr. Long stared. "Out of . . . line?"

"That's right. Sorry, but the Army makes its own bricks."

"Well, by golly . . ." Mr. Long smiled broadly. "Er . . . thanks a lot, Salty."

"For what?"

J.P. laughed. "For not needing bricks, sir."

The soldier scratched his head as the man and boy ran back to the lead wagon and quickly drove the small caravan away.

On a side street Winchester Long halted the mules and wiped his brow with a bright-red handkerchief. "By gosh, boy," he said in a low voice. "How'd you know the Army doesn't buy bricks?"

"My father said they never buy what they can make, sir. And I remembered them making bricks at Fort Bowie."

"By gosh! Boy, I owe you ten years of my life. Anything you want, you just name it!"

"Well, there is one thing . . ."

"Say it and hang the cost!"

"Well, sir . . ." Suddenly J.P. felt bashful. "I guess I'd be real glad to see that farmer get back his wagon and corn."

Mr. Long stared. "You know about him?"

"Yes."

"Well, I'll be darned." He scratched one ear thoughtfully. "All right. Tonight after I unload the bricks, I'll reload his corn and give it to him in the morning. That'll keep me busy all night—but like I said, anything you want."

"About the other two wagons . . ."

"I won them fair and square." He looked at J.P. then quickly looked away again. "Well, almost fair and square."

"Could you give them back too?"

"Both?"

"Well, sir . . ."

"I'll give back one. And pay cash for the other, all right? Then I'll drive it to California. I hear San Francisco is a place of opportunity—for someone like me, that is."

"Wonderful," exclaimed J.P. "I'll even bring you a traveling companion."

"Rather make it by myself, boy. I'm what folks call a loner."

"Except that my friend badly needs a ride."

"Hmm."

"He has no money to share expenses," continued J.P. excitedly. "But he'll sure be company."

"Hmm."

"Of course, he'll probably spend all his time in back under the canvas. Seems he can't stand dust."

"You call that being company?"

"Will you do it, sir?"

"Well . . ." Winchester Long sighed. "Since you want it, all right."

"Yes, sir. And like you said, when you talk you make anyone believe anything."

"That's true, boy."

"Maybe before you leave you can talk around town. You know, to make folks think it was all a mistake about Uncle Perez and me selling guns to the Indians."

Winchester Long chuckled. "I'll sure enough do that, boy. Come this time two days from now you'd better have a helper in that store. Business will be that good."

"Thank you, Mr. Long. And now . . ."

"Something *else?*"

"No, sir," J.P. replied quickly. "That is—well, I just hope you'll somehow stay clear of trouble. You see, Mr. Long, I can't help liking you a lot."

Winchester Long pulled out the red handkerchief again and loudly blew his nose. Then he wiped his eyes and cleared his throat. "Boy, you can bet I'll do my best," he said in a husky voice.

"Thanks." Grinning, J.P. jumped down to the ground. "I'll have my friend look for you."

"Right, boy. Somewhere on the main drag. And if you ever make it to San Francisco, be sure to hunt me out. I think you and I could be real good friends."

"Thank you, sir. I feel the same way."

With a happy wave of his hand, J.P. ran in search of Harrison Tulip.

At about 3 P.M. the next day the stagecoach came roaring into town. The man with the red whiskers waved as he passed the store. Aunt Martha agreed to take J.P.'s place in the store while he ran to the stage station for news from Fort Bowie. His closing the store the day before was never even mentioned.

There was news all right. Firechin Tom didn't even finish unhitching the horses before taking J.P. to one side. His face was very serious. J.P. felt his heart sink like a stone.

"Is my mother all right?" asked J.P. in a tight voice.

"Fine," replied Firechin Tom.

"And Pepe and Maria?"

"Also fine."

"Then . . ." The word came from him like a sigh. "It's about my father, isn't it? The word has finally come through . . ."

"There was that, yes. Seems a group of armed Mexicans saw recent signs where someone'd camped near a deserted mine. If it *was* Donegal Dan, then the news is good."

Please God make it so, the boy prayed silently.

"But, J.P., I've also got bad news. A few nights ago there was an Indian raid. Nothing big, just some horse stealing. They hit the civilian corral and got a few horses." He turned away. "Afraid they also got a burro."

J.P. felt sick. "B-Bravo?"

Firechin Tom nodded. For a moment there was only emptiness inside the boy. He could think of nothing to say. He felt numb all over.

"Tom?"

"Sure, J.P."

"You driving right back to Fort Bowie?"

"Not for another week, I'm afraid. Got to take some dispatches to Fort Yuma."

"I see." J.P. took a deep breath. "Then thanks."

He started to walk away.

"J.P.?"

The boy stopped.

"I'm awful sorry, you know that."

"Sure."

"And your mom says—well, I guess you know how she feels."

"Sure."

Nothing counted now, nothing at all. Nothing except Bravo who would soon be Sunday dinner for some meat-hungry Apache.

Suddenly Tucson was a deadweight pressing on him. Right then and there he made up his mind. Tonight would be his last night here.

There wasn't much hope for Bravo. But what little there was depended on—he took a deep breath—on a future desert scout named Juanito Patrick Mendoza O'Flynn.

13

Home Again

Four nights later a long row of loaded supply wagons sat on the parade ground at Fort Bowie. Although the night was moonless, stars shone brightly enough to cast a silvery haze on the ground.

The canvas backing on one wagon lifted slowly, and J.P. stuck out his head. There were guards around the wagons, of course. Now if he could just avoid them . . .

He climbed out and his foot scraped the ground. He waited. When he heard nothing, he started to run.

"Halt!" snapped a voice from close by.

J.P. became stiff as a brass cannon.

"Who goes there?" yelled the guard.

The boy slipped behind a wagon wheel. From the darkness he heard a rifle bolt spring home. His mouth turned to cotton.

"Last chance," yelled the soldier. "Who goes there?"

"It's me, ya' darned fool," said a second voice.

"Who's *me?*"

"Your barracks mate Private Tessy, that's who." The second voice was annoyed. "What's the matter with you?"

"I thought I heard something."

"Sure you did. You heard me."

"Sorry," said the first voice. "Guess I've got jitters tonight."

"Guess you sure enough have."

The two men talked about Colonel Blunt's last Saturday morning inspection. Both had been found with their shoes unpolished and now were walking guard duty for punishment.

J.P. waited until their voices drifted away, then on the run he took off again. One more obstacle–the wooden palisade surrounding the fort. At night the main gate was always locked. But he knew a place where with some luck a boy could make it over the wall.

He chose a dark corner and dropped ten feet into soft sand. Brushing himself off, he grinned; this part seemed easy after that awful trip from Tucson.

He'd ridden all the way in a wagon loaded with Army boots. Luckily he'd brought enough water, plus a few packages of dried beef. But it had been terribly hot beneath that canvas. And once, when the wagons had circled to fight off an Indian attack, he'd almost run out with the screaming meemies. But now J.P. was almost home.

The nervous neighing of horses informed him that he'd reached the civilian corral. That made his heart ache for Bravo so badly that his legs became as weak as old rope. He found his house completely dark. For a while he sat in the starlight, listening to the great quietness of the desert. Suddenly he realized he was afraid to go inside.

How angry would Mamacita be because he'd run away? How hurt would she feel that he'd come back? He sat in the darkness a long time. Once or twice he wondered if it wouldn't be better to just continue on into the desert. But he was too tired. It seemed a year since he had slept on anything softer than leather-soled Army boots.

He climbed up to the barred window space close to his bed. By squeezing and pushing and squeezing some more, he finally made his way inside the house.

His bed was near the wall. If he could just . . .

"Don't move!"

Wearily J.P. thought how many times he had recently heard that command. He waited until a lantern glowed brightly in the darkness.

Mamacita held a shotgun aimed in his direction.

"Hello, Mamá," he said.

With a loud cry she set down the gun and lantern and rushed at him. She gripped him so tightly that J.P. could hardly breathe. But he didn't care. Even if she squeezed him to death he wouldn't care.

"Juanito," she cried softly. "My boy has come home. . . ."

If he still had any doubts about being welcome at home, what happened next made him forget them completely. Because that's when Pepe and Maria ran into the room. They yelled and howled and laughed and beat him on the back with sheer joy. Right then and there J.P. O'Flynn decided he was the happiest boy in the West.

Very early the next morning he "borrowed" a horse from the corral and rode out to the pile of stones that he and Natanah used for signaling. After building a message he returned to Fort Bowie and slipped back into the house.

After that he waited impatiently for time to pass. Mostly he stayed indoors, not wanting to meet people from the fort. Then, two days later at dawn, he again sneaked out of the house. Once more it was necessary to take a horse from the corral. He knew he was doing something wrong, but how else could he get out to the desert on time? Anyway, Bravo's life was at stake.

This time he chose Mr. Christensen's black mare. Riding bareback, he galloped into the desert. At the stones, Natanah's message told him that the Apache boy would be waiting at the usual place. J.P. reached the secret place about three hours before high noon. This time Natanah wasn't hiding. His black eyes sparkled gaily at the sight of his friend.

"It has been a long time, Ish-kay-nay."

"Too long, Natanah."

The Apache boy eyed the familiar black mare. "You stole her?"

"Yes."

"Good for you."

J.P. shrugged; there wasn't time to explain. "Natanah, do you know about Bravo?"

The Indian boy grinned. "He's a terrible coward, that burro."

"You've seen him?"

"Yes. Quick Killer keeps him in the corral."

J.P. groaned. "Natanah, you've got to get him back for me."

"Back?"

"Please. Steal him for me."

The Apache shook his head proudly. "I'm sorry. But my people do not steal from each other. Quick Killer took your burro in a raid; now it is his."

J.P. restrained his temper. "You can buy him from Quick Killer. I'll bring you the money."

"White man's money means nothing to Apaches."

"Then blankets–anything he wants."

"Quick Killer has many blankets. I'm sorry, Ish-kay-nay. All he wants is the burro."

J.P.'s face grew stern. "Then I'll find your camp and steal him myself."

"You make a joke, my friend."

"No joke."

Natanah's eyes narrowed. "You mean this?"

"I certainly do!"

Natanah shook his head. "It is only a burro. A lazy, stupid burro. If you are captured by my people, it could mean torture and death. Why should you risk that for a mere burro?"

"Burro! Burro!" exclaimed J.P. angrily. "Can't you see that he's my friend? I love him, that's why."

Natanah didn't understand. It was not the way of his people to feel strongly about animals.

J.P. said, "Will you tell me the location of your camp?"

"No, Ish-kay-nay. That is strongly forbidden."

"Then I will find it myself."

"On this stolen horse?"

"On foot if necessary!"

The Apache boy was troubled. J.P.'s mind was obviously made up. Yet Natanah knew that what his friend planned was very dangerous. "There has been talk," he said, "about a wounded white man seen on the desert near our mountains. Some of our braves have searched for him, but he manages to hide. I do not know for sure if this is true. But if so, why not wait and see if it is your father?"

"Will Quick Killer wait that long to eat Bravo?"

Reluctantly Natanah shook his head. "No. Soon the braves will hold a fierce war dance. There will be a feast, and the burro will be cooked."

"So I'll just have to rescue him before then."

Natanah scowled and kicked angrily at the sand. "I'll tell you why you can't get your animal back. First you have to go to those mountains." He pointed to a row of peaks in the south. "On foot, you say. Yet even on a horse you could get no farther than the foothills. There an Apache sentry will see you. He will light a signal fire. Then those in the main camp will answer with smoke of their own.

"A war party will try to find you. Somehow you will have to hide from them. For food you will have to find the three-arm saguaro trees marked with an arrow. And even if you reach our mountains, you will have to find the trail that runs between the two finger rocks. Then you must make your way up to the camp without being seen. Think of all these things, Ish-kay-nay. Maybe then you'll see that the burro is not worth such a risk."

J.P. tried to keep his face blank. But he knew that Natanah had purposely given him information that would help to find the Apache camp.

Natanah scowled. "You will still try?"

"Yes. Tomorrow morning I'll start."

"You know I can't help you? Even if you're captured, there will be nothing I can do."

"I understand."

"Then may Yusn the Life-giver watch over you on your journey," Natanah said gravely. "May He protect you from the desert and from our warriors."

They touched hands.

"Ish-kay-nay, will we look today for adventure?"

"I'm sorry, Natanah. But not today." It wasn't a time for fun. The moments left in Bravo's life were too few.

"I understand. But remember—no matter where or when we meet again, we will always be friends. Never will I try to kill you. Good-bye, Ish-kay-nay."

He mounted his pony, waved once, and galloped away. J.P. sadly turned homeward.

14

A Long Journey

He was up before dawn with his mind racing. No use borrowing another horse, not unless he was ready really to steal—which he wasn't.

He had gone to bed fully dressed. Now he awakened Pepe.

"Shh," warned J.P. "Just listen to me, little brother. I'll tell you where I'm going and what you must tell Mamá."

Then he spoke in a quick whisper. When he had finished, Pepe said breathlessly, "Can I go with you?"

"Of course not."

"Why not?"

"Because . . ." Then J.P. decided not to tell his brother

that he was too little. "Because you're needed here, Pepe. You're the man of this house again."

That made Pepe feel too proud to argue. With a final good-bye, J.P. grunted his way through the window bars and dropped to the ground. The chill of night made him shiver. He glanced upward and the position of the stars told him it was very early indeed. His heart pounded strongly. But it skipped a beat when something moved in the darkness. J.P. stepped closer and suddenly couldn't believe his eyes.

A horse. He felt for the stirrups and knew they were Apache. This was Natanah's pony. He grinned happily. Sometime during the night his friend had brought him this gift.

Thank you, Natanah . . .

He traveled fast, moving southward toward the red star in the constellation Scorpio. Grayness finally washed the eastern sky, and by then Scorpio was lying on its head. He was surprised that he had already traveled almost three hours. When full dawn came, he saw that he'd ridden almost half the distance to the southern mountains.

He found the first Apache food cache. It was under an ancient three-armed saguaro taller than all others. He was so hungry that even the dried cactus strips hidden inside a rawhide bag tasted good. For water he cut open a small barrel cactus with a stone knife he had brought from home. He sucked on the soggy pulp until his throat felt moist.

The taste wasn't particularly good, but out here that small amount of wetness meant the difference between living and dying of thirst.

He let the pony lick at the cactus too. Now he had a decision to make. They were deep inside Apache country. Dust raised by the pony's hooves was certain to be seen by an Apache sentry. J.P. decided to set the pony free. It would most probably find its way back to Natanah's camp.

After the pony trotted away, J.P. remembered what his father had taught him, and he holed up inside a small rock cave. After a while he even managed to fall asleep. Four or five times he came awake and returned to sleep again. When night finally arrived, he knew it was again time to travel.

Now he felt terribly hungry. He was also very nervous. For no good reason, he thought, since the nighttimes were fairly safe from Apaches. Then, a few hours later, he almost stepped on a rattlesnake. He never saw it, he just heard its dry rattle near his feet.

He continued walking. But now his imagination insisted on playing tricks, and he felt he was being followed. He stopped to listen and heard nothing but the wind. He walked on. Again he had the sensation of being stalked.

There was one way to find out. Moving silently, J.P. stepped back the way he'd come. His scalp prickled–at any moment he expected to bump into the sinewy form of an Apache. But no one was there. He thought of the Apache bogeyman, the thing Natanah called the Gray

Clown. It was an evil spirit that Chiricahua children were taught to fear. Since this was Chiricahua country, J.P. wondered whether the Gray Clown was perhaps something he should worry about too.

Let's face it, he thought. Out alone at night, even a future desert scout was entitled to feel nervous.

After daybreak he found another food cache. He ate hungrily, then sucked more barrel-cactus pulp and studied his situation. The mountains were much closer now. He could see timber on the highest crests. And high up on the slopes, jutting out like fingers, were the two grayish finger rocks.

Where in all that rock, brush, and trees would the Apache camp be located? Apache guards would be lurking on those rocky foothills. J.P. studied the brownish-red hills and selected one he considered most likely to shelter the lookout. After a deep breath and a silent prayer, he stepped out to the desert floor.

And started to dance.

He kicked up his heels, leaped, swung himself sideways and kept time to the tune of "Old Dan Tucker."

> "Old Dan Tucker came to town
> Ridin' a billy goat and draggin' a hound . . ."

Soon he had raised enough dust to be seen from the mountaintops themselves. To make sure, he ran a race with an imaginary jackrabbit. He circled his rock shelter, scuffing his feet and raising more dust. Then he crept back into the rocks to watch.

The smoke signal puffed up about five minutes later. It billowed upward in a sudden black cloud from the very hill he had guessed as the lookout location. Carefully he searched for the reply. When it came, he marked the spot with his eyes.

Good. From his left, closer than he dared to hope. According to Natanah, that second signal came from the site of the main Apache camp. Suddenly small specks of dust rose from the reddish hill. When they were closer he realized that two or three braves were riding out to investigate.

He slid between two close rocks. The space was so tight that his breath felt warm on his face. Finally he heard them. They followed his footprints to the rocks. He heard them scuffling close by, and once the rock against which he pressed vibrated as someone walked on it. The Apaches were directly over his head. He didn't dare come out until after dark. Then, when he found the Apaches gone, he almost yelled with relief.

That night he traveled again. His muscles ached, and his feet hurt. Time and again he wished he hadn't come. But different thoughts pushed him on, thoughts of Donegal Dan and the belief that this trip was a testing of all his father had taught him. And he remembered Natanah, who probably did not really believe a white boy could make the long, dangerous trip up to the Apache camp. And because

of Bravo. And he kept also going because he was just plain stubborn.

He didn't feel like walking another step. But walk he did, this time uphill into the mountains—one step after another until his head ached sharply. But now there was grass under his feet and he moved silently. There were also trees. The air grew cooler as the mountain trail took him higher.

He traveled uphill so long that he finally wondered if he was lost. Then the ground dipped forward, the grass became higher, and for one moment J.P. was moving downhill instead of up. That's when he saw the weird-glowing lights.

For a moment he didn't believe the sight. It was like seeing great round eyes staring up at him through the darkness. The yellowish-blue lights neither flickered nor moved. He felt the hairs rise on his neck.

Only his great curiosity allowed him to step closer. Then he saw that the cold lights were not fires at all, but the glowing tops of rotten tree stumps.

He grinned nervously. Yes, this too he'd heard about from his father. It was called fox fire, and his father said the stuff glowed with the same kind of light as fireflies. He touched a glowing stump; his hand shone in the darkness until he rubbed it clean on a patch of grass.

What a crazy time to explore, he thought suddenly. He turned and again began walking uphill. But not for long. Perhaps twenty minutes more, and then something dead ahead made him stop in his tracks.

More fire. A hot one this time. The leaping flames of a campfire. And around it he saw the outlines of many people.

With heart-stopping suddenness J.P. realized he had reached the Apache camp.

15

Captured!

Suddenly he was scared. It was one thing to imagine oneself at the Chiricahua camp, but something entirely different to *be* there. Crouching behind a rock he stared toward that great circle of fire. Apaches—and so gosh-darn many of them!

They were really whooping it up, too . . . probably that war dance. Two or three braves wore hideous masks that made them look like monsters. One taller than the rest wore a captured soldier's uniform and a mask even more awful than the others. J.P. had a feeling that this was the mean old medicine man Natanah had told him about.

Apache braves sat around the circle smoking clay pipes.

About six feet behind them sat the women. There was shouting and singing, and the beating of sticks against animal hides. And always the shrill sounds of nose flutes.

It was a war dance, all right. The Chiricahuas were making ready for a big raid somewhere. That meant four nights of singing and dancing—no telling how many nights it had been going on so far—followed by a feast, which was probably when Quick Killer and his friends hoped to eat their fill of burro meat . . .

J.P.'s heart thumped wildly. Maybe he was crazy to come up here. But now that he *was* here he had better find the animal corral—*and fast*. On hands and knees he crawled away. The ground was rough, and the sounds of Apache drums and shrill voices beat against his ears like the growls of angry wolves.

He crawled into a cluster of wickiups, those brush huts in which the Apaches lived. Wisps of smoke curled up from small holes in their tops. Now and then he caught the pungent scent of burning sage. As he moved past one wickiup, a small figure suddenly popped out of the entance and stared at him.

Fright hit J.P.'s stomach like an ax. It was an Apache boy about three years old, a fat-cheeked, nut-brown boy who stared at him with eyes that became as round as silver dollars.

With a loud squeal the fat little boy dived back inside. J.P. scrambled to one wall and hid.

"The Gray Clown," the little boy yelled. "Outside."

"*Kah-kay-nay.*" A female voice laughed. "You're a frightened rabbit."

"*Shee-dah-trih!*" yelled the little boy again. "I myself saw!"

Flickering firelight fell from the interior of the wickiup as someone lifted its rawhide door.

"*Todahdrah, ta-Shis-Inday,*" said the girl's voice again. "Nothing there. Only Chiricahuas."

She went back inside. J.P. swallowed hard and moved on.

On hands and knees he circled the Apache camp, keeping to those places where the grass was high. Suddenly he heard the neighing of a horse. Over there . . . the corral? He raised his head to look.

Yes, there was a group of ponies behind a fence of sapling logs. Was Bravo there too? He crept closer. "Bravo," he whispered loudly as he dared. "Bravo—you hear me?"

No reply. He crept still closer. Some Indian ponies neighed nervously.

"Bravo?"

From deep in that crowd of animals came the sweet, wonderful, rusty sound:

"*Hee-aww! Hee-a-a-a-w!*"

J.P. felt like shouting with joy. But suddenly he heard approaching voices. He flung himself on his belly and closed his eyes. If only they didn't step on him . . .

"We must hurry," said one man's voice. "The fire signal

says Cochise approaches. He must not think his people do not welcome him."

"Listen," said the other. "That crazy burro also welcomes our great chief."

"Let him howl," said the first man. "Soon his voice will be silent in our bellies."

They laughed. J.P. raised his head and saw them open the corral gate. A few moments later they rode past him and disappeared toward the campfire.

J.P. crept into the corral. Frightened by his scent, the Indian ponies scurried away. Suddenly a small gray figure with a cold nose rushed up to him.

"Bravo," whispered J.P. happily.

The donkey almost collapsed with joy. "No time for that," J.P. whispered. "Come on, let's get out of here. And please–*be quiet* . . ."

The burro shivered. J.P. clutched a handful of gray hairs and led him out of the corral.

It took him a moment to get his bearings. Over there, then behind the big fire. Back that way through the grass. Then if he could just find the trail that led down the mountain toward the finger rocks . . .

They moved so slowly that his legs became cramped. When they passed through the rows of wickiups, J.P. felt sure that someone would hear his heart pounding. Then they passed the fire, where the chants and drums and flutes and yelling voices turned the night into a bedlam of sound. The masked figures danced faster now. The tall shaman in the soldier's uniform looked like an awful demon, and J.P. shoved Bravo's head to one side so the burro wouldn't faint at that frightening sight.

Then they reached the trail that went down the mountain. If only they could hurry for the next fifteen minutes they'd stand a chance . . .

But Bravo stumbled. He didn't really fall, he only tripped forward. But the burro's nerves were so worn that he couldn't hold back the loud bray of fear that poured from his throat. J.P. felt rooted to the spot. The burro's voice was louder than anything he had ever heard before.

"*Please,* Bravo! No more . . ."

Too late. He heard the rushing of moccasins behind him, smelled the deer marrow with which Apaches greased their hair. Sinewy arms encircled his throat and he was lifted from the ground.

"What is happening?" yelled an Apache voice.

"My burro!" answered another. J.P. shuddered at Quick Killer's snarling voice. "And a White-eye!"

"White-eye!"

"*White-eye American!*"

The hated words were passed from one to another like an angry echo.

"Quick! Bring him to the fire!"

J.P. was dragged through the night to the fire, where an entire camp of angrily shouting Apaches milled and shoved to look at him.

The dancing stopped. They shouted angry questions. Their shouts rang in J.P.'s ears.

"Just a boy!"

"No—a young *man!*"

"How did he get here?"

"Is he crazy?"

"What was he doing?"

"Stealing a burro!"

"Stealing—from *us?*"

Their shouted questions and answers were hurled at him without pause. Several squaws shook war clubs under his nose. One fat woman with puffy eyes waved a club so close to his head that Quick Killer grabbed her arm.

"Thank you," J.P. told him in perfect Apache.

That started them yelling questions again.

"Save him for Cochise," someone shouted. "It will amuse our great chief to torture him."

But Quick Killer had other ideas. It was his burro that had been stolen, which made it his privilege to claim J.P. as a captive. He tied the boy's hands behind him. Then J.P. was marched toward Quick Killer's wickiup.

No sign of Natanah. With deep despair J.P. considered the grave possibility that these were the last moments of his very, very short life.

16

Death at Dawn

The entrance to Quick Killer's wickiup was so low that even J.P. had to stoop to get in. The air inside was heavy with the pungent smell of the sage fire glowing on the floor. He also smelled the dried grass and brush of the wickiup walls, and the scent of foods that he didn't recognize.

Dirt was packed around the base of the wickiup, and there were grass mats on the ground. Deerhide robes covered grass beds. He saw baskets, unpainted clay pots, gourds hanging from the ceiling poles, hair ropes and—surprising considering Quick Killer's fierceness—a one-stringed violin near the door.

And by the fire—a giant iron stewpot. J.P.'s eyes bulged: *Was this the pot that would hold Bravo?*

Two women, including the fat squaw who had threatened him outside, glared angrily at him. J.P. was shoved to the floor while Quick Killer towered over him with eyes blazing, his knee-length moccasins turned down to show the hilt of a long-bladed knife.

"You speak Chiricahua?" snapped Quick Killer.

"Yes."

"Then answer. Why did you come?"

"To g-get Bravo."

"To get what?"

"My b-burro."

The Apache brave snarled. "*My* burro."

"You stole him from me."

"And you would steal him back?"

J.P. nodded.

"How did you get past our sentries?" asked Quick Killer.

"By traveling at night."

"Alone?"

"Yes."

"On foot?"

"Yes."

"A lie!" shouted the two squaws at the same moment. The mean-looking woman said, "No White-eye can cross the desert on foot."

"Can a Chiricahua?" asked J.P.

"Of course."

"Then so can I," the boy replied with force. "I am the son of a white scout. I can do whatever the Chiricahuas do."

Quick Killer grinned nastily. "Except steal a burro."

"Next time I'll get away."

"No next time," said the Apache, and the squaws laughed. "On your feet!"

J.P. stood up. His hands were bound too tightly and they hurt. Outside, the drums, flutes and singing had started again.

"I will take you back to the fire," Quick Killer said. "Soon Cochise will come. From him I will ask permission to kill you."

The squaws pushed J.P. outside. They shoved him toward the ringed circle around the fire. Quick Killer sat the boy on the ground and squatted next to him. For a moment the dancing hesitated as everyone looked uneasily toward the white boy. Then the masked dancing, clapping of hands, smoking of pipes–and, he noticed for the first time, the drinking of fermented mescal–continued.

The masks were of stiffened hides covered with paints, and decorated with horns and feathers. The shaman in the soldier's uniform danced wildly, shaking rattles and holding his medicine bag close to his chest. A few minutes of watching told J.P. several things.

This was a big medicine dance, all right. It was to bring great luck in hunting and war. He also saw that most of the braves disliked the old medicine man in the soldier's uniform. They seemed afraid of him. A moment later J.P. found out why.

The tall figure danced directly in front of him. The mask covered its face and part of its chest, a gruesome thing that resembled a wolf's head. The dancing figure reeked of fermented mescal juice. Suddenly it pointed a rattle at J.P.'s head and yelled:

"Death to the White-eye!"

The others shouted approval.

"Slow death!" yelled the shaman.

"*Ay-yee*," screamed the others approvingly.

"On an ant hill!"

"*Ay-yee* . . ."

"Or roasted over a fire!"

"*Ay-yee* . . ."

Quick Killer grinned. "I agree, mighty Medicine Man. Death to all who would steal from Quick Killer."

"*Ay-yee* . . ." screamed the others, the squaws louder than everyone else. J.P. fought to hold back his tears. He would try to die like a scout. But *pain*—that was too much, even for Bravo's sake.

That stupid burro! he thought indignantly. *If he'd only kept his big mouth shut this wouldn't have happened.* Suddenly J.P. became angry, and when he did . . .

The Imp popped into his head.

The shaman shook a long-handled rattle at him. "Death to the White-eye!"

"*Ay-yee . . .*"

"Death by the knife!"

"*Ay-yee . . .*"

J.P. lifted one foot and kicked the rattle from the shaman's hand. Suddenly around the fire there was a dead silence.

"You make too much noise," J.P. told the medicine man. "And you smell bad, too."

Someone laughed. Then someone else, and suddenly they were all laughing. Their roars and shouts and squeals rang through the night. Here and there a brave flopped on his back howling. Even Quick Killer chuckled silently.

"Death to the white boy!" shouted the shaman, louder than before. But this time no one shouted approval.

"Be careful, old man," someone yelled. "The white boy might kick you to death."

Suddenly the shaman pulled a knife from his belt. He raised it high. Firelight glinted against the blade. J.P. closed his eyes. This time the gosh-darned Imp had gotten him into the worst trouble of all. . . .

But the blade did not fall. When J.P. finally dared open his eyes, everyone was staring at a very tall Indian looking down from a white horse.

"Chochise," ran the whisper. "Cochise has come. . . ."

Quick Killer ran to the chief. Others joined them. J.P. saw them speaking but could not hear their words. After a while Cochise rode off with some of his men, including J.P.'s captor.

The dancing continued.

It went on for a long time, and now the American boy was almost ignored. The shaman in the wolf-head mask finally grew weary and left the fire ring. Then Quick Killer came back, lifted J.P. to his feet, and dragged him back to the wickiup.

Cochise and four elderly men sat waiting. The chief was taller than all others, with black piercing eyes that seemed to stare right into J.P.'s head.

"It is true you came to steal the burro?" he asked in a deep voice.

"Yes, sir," replied J.P.

"You crossed the desert on foot? And alone?"

"Yes."

"How far?"

"*Ah-han-day*, a long way. From Fort Bowie."

"How?"

"By traveling only at night. By eating Apache food hidden beneath the marked saguaro trees. By drinking from barrel cactus. And by following the smoke signals until I found this place."

There was a long moment of silence.

"Where did you learn these things?" asked Cochise.

"From my father. He is a long-haired scout."

"How old are you?"

"*Nah-kee-sah-tah*. Twelve."

The glowing black eyes flicked over the others. "Just a boy."

"But old enough to shoot a rifle," snapped Quick Killer.

"A very brave boy," said Cochise, and some of the subchiefs nodded.

"All the more reason to kill him," said Quick Killer. "He came to steal from me, Cochise. For that reason I ask for his life. It is the Chiricahua way to kill their enemies."

"True," said Cochise. "But once it was not the way. Once the Chiricahua and white men were friends."

"But not now," Quick Killer said with growing anger. "That is why I demand what is rightfully mine. His life!"

Cochise was silent a moment. "Take the boy back to the fire," he said softly. "We will discuss this thing and decide."

"*Anah-zont-tee!*" ordered Quick Killer, and J.P. stood up. The man who was now his worst enemy returned him to the fire and left him there.

The shaman in the blue uniform was dancing more fiercely than ever. He shook rattles at J.P. and yelled for the white boy's death. The others began to respond again. J.P. decided the shaman was very drunk, although it seemed something was wrong. He could no longer catch the reek of mescal from the tall figure. How come?

The brightly colored wolf-head mask frightened him. For some reason it looked even more terrible now than before. The shaman was dancing faster. He no longer seemed to be an old man. Now he was just a bloodthirsty savage howling for his death.

Quick Killer returned. He stepped close to the fire and

raised his hands. The shaman stopped dancing. The drums became silent, the yelling voices died away.

"It has been decided," Quick Killer yelled. "The chiefs have voted." He looked at J.P. and grinned. "The white boy dies!"

The drums throbbed, the voices chanted, the shaman danced. J.P. dropped his head and looked down at the dirt.

No, he would not let them see him cry. But, oh gosh! How badly he wished he had never left Tucson!

17

The Shaman Unmasked

Quick Killer dragged J.P. back to the wickiup and flung him inside. Cochise and the subchiefs were gone.

"You will die when the sun rises," said the fierce Apache. "Right before we begin to feast. Until then you can sit and think how foolish you were to try to steal from Quick Killer."

With a nasty grin the scar-faced warrior left him to rejoin the dancing. J.P. sat miserably on the dirt floor, his hands bound behind him. The squaws sat scowling. With each burst of laughter outside their scowls became worse. Having to watch this white captive was making them miss all the fun.

Then the sounds outside changed. They could hear angry voices. One was Quick Killer's, shrill and harsh. The other was equally angry. One of the squaws lifted the door flap to look.

"It is our husband," she said excitedly to the other woman. "You hear? He argues with the shaman. I think the medicine man demanded the captured burro to eat."

"The shaman is old," sneered the second wife of Quick Killer. "He has no teeth. Why should he want to eat meat?"

"Listen," said the first. "It sounds like they will soon fight. That is bad, my sister. It is not good to fight with a medicine man."

The second woman shrugged. "Maybe then our husband will become shaman. I would not mind that."

There was a sudden burst of yelling.

"There they go," said the squaw from the doorway. "Quick Killer is chasing the medicine man into the brush. I think he wants to kill him. All the Chiricahuas are following. . . ."

She turned quickly. "Can't we go see, my sister?"

"Who will watch the prisoner?"

"His hands are tied. We can bind him to the wall . . ."

The shouts outside grew wild with excitement.

"Hurry, my sister," said the first squaw. "We will miss all the fun."

"The drunken fools," scowled the second squaw. But with a piece of rawhide she bound J.P.'s arms to a sapling in the wickiup wall. She tested it, then she and the other squaw lumbered out to join the crowd.

J.P. heard the noises fade into the distance. He wondered how long it would be until dawn. Suddenly the deerskin over the entrance flapped back.

"Hello, Ish-kay-nay."

The voice whispered quickly, and a copper-colored face flashed a sudden grin.

"Natanah . . ."

With quick steps the Apache boy crossed the floor. He slashed the rawhide bonds from J.P.'s wrists. J.P. rubbed his wrists briskly, wincing with pain.

"Here," said Natanah, throwing a bundle at J.P.'s feet. "Apache clothes. Put them on—*fast!*"

J.P. stripped. He slid into a long-sleeved buckskin shirt. He tied the broad loincloth that reached to above his knees. Then he slid into the knee-length moccasins. Natanah pulled a wide strip of red flannel from his belt and tied it around J.P.'s forehead. Then the Apache boy stepped back and examined J.P. by firelight.

"Never have I seen such an awful Apache," said Natanah with a grin. "But in the darkness perhaps you can pass. Come—*quickly*."

He led J.P. outside. The white boy tried to thank his friend, but Natanah motioned him to silence. A few steps, and suddenly J.P. halted.

"Bravo," he said. "I can't leave without him."

"You want to die?"

"No. But I don't want him to die either."

Natanah hesitated. For a moment J.P. thought he would leave him there. J.P. wouldn't blame his friend; Natanah had already risked his life for him tonight.

"All right. I will take you to your burro."

They crawled back to the corral. Bravo came when J.P. called him. Before he could bray his joy, J.P. took the rawhide rope that had bound his hands and looped it around the burro's mouth. It would not prevent him from making noise, but it might remind him to try to keep his mouth shut.

Natanah led them through the darkness to the trail which wound down the mountain. He moved so quickly that J.P. had trouble keeping up with him. Behind at the camp they heard the sounds of returning voices.

"I wonder if Quick Killer killed that shaman," whispered J.P.

"Don't worry about the medicine man," Natanah whispered back. "You would be surprised at how well he can take care of himself."

The trail was steep, and they had to move slowly. J.P.'s heart throbbed with excitement and joy. Not only was his life being saved, but Bravo was escaping that iron stewpot! Natanah waited for them to catch up with him. "I will take you only a little way farther, Ish-kay-nay. Then I must go somewhere alone and think." The Apache boy's voice was very sad.

"Think?"

"Yes. Whether or not I have betrayed my people. If so, then I must ask for punishment."

J.P. swallowed hard. "Natanah, I feel awful."

"Don't. I would do it again for my friend . . ." Natanah looked at Bravo and smiled. "For my *friends*. Even so, if I have done wrong I must be punished."

"*Punished for what, boy?*"

The voice was deep. J.P. gasped at the tall figure that suddenly appeared on the trail ahead.

Natanah swung around.

"*Natan-in-jah* . . ." he said with awe in his voice. "Great Chief . . ."

Cochise stepped closer. His hand grasped J.P. under the chin and lifted his head upward.

"The white boy," said Cochise and turned to Natanah. "You said your friend?"

"Yes, Great Chief."

"What is your name?"

"Natanah–Cornflower. A weak name, Great Chief. But I have tried to be stronger than my name."

"You helped him to escape?"

"I did . . ."

There was a long moment of silence. Then the tall figure said, "Tell me how this boy became your friend."

In a hushed voice Natanah told Cochise everything. Not once did the chief interrupt. Behind them from the camp they heard angry shouting. J.P.'s escape had been discovered.

Natanah finished telling of his visits with J.P., and how they shared each others' lives and secrets.

"The white boy was very brave to come to the Apache camp," said Cochise tonelessly. "Even braver than some of my warriors. And you, Chiricahua boy—you are loyal to your friend and that too is good."

His hand reached out to touch Natanah's shoulder. "In my mind you bear a new name. From tonight on I will no longer think of you as Cornflower. To me you will be known as"—he smiled—"*Strong Friend.* When the time is right, I will tell all the Chiricahua people of your new name."

"Thank you, great Cochise." The voice of Natanah—or Strong Friend now—shook with great pride. "But have I done wrong to our people?"

"One never does wrong helping a friend."

"But—I think our people are searching for my friend. Will you make him a prisoner again?"

"I must, even though I voted against his death." Cochise's voice was very firm. "I cannot help one of our enemy to escape. Unless, of course, I suddenly heard a noise in the brush and went to investigate. Then I could not see the white boy escape. . . ."

The tall figure slowly turned. "Listen closely, Strong Friend. Do you hear a sound in the brush? Perhaps a sound like that of a mountain lion creeping toward our horses?"

"It seems that I do," said Strong Friend seriously.

"Then I had better find the lion before it does harm.

And you, Strong Friend, make haste. Our people are indeed on your trail."

The tall figure disappeared into the underbrush. Strong Friend began running, J.P. and Bravo followed closely after him. The howls behind them became louder.

Bravo was again frightened and tried to bray with his mouth closed. It was a terrible sound, but J.P. did not try to stop him. The sound did not matter now. The pursuing Apaches knew exactly where the boys and burro were.

Their situation was desperate—so the Imp popped into J.P.'s head.

"Over here!" he suddenly yelled. He changed direction and plunged into the brush, almost dragging Bravo with him.

"I have never come this way," Strong Friend breathed by his side. "It does not lead down the mountain."

But J.P. plunged straight ahead. Suddenly the underbrush cleared and before them glowed the tree stumps ringed with fox fire.

The Apache boy stopped dead.

"What is this place?" His voice shook.

"Haven't you been here before?"

"No. The shaman has called this place taboo. Apaches are not allowed here." He trembled. "It frightens me, Ish-kay-nay . . ."

J.P. grabbed a handful of the glowing moss, then yanked Bravo's tail. The donkey squealed with pain and surprise.

Another handful of evil-smelling moss, and this time J.P. grabbed the burro by his ears.

Then the bushes were trampled by many feet and the pursuing Apaches entered the clearing.

J.P. leaped on Bravo's back. He screamed at the top of his voice and jabbed the terrified burro forward, and aimed him directly at the Apaches.

Before Strong Friend ducked out of sight, he suddenly understood. The silence of his people told him what it was they saw: a howling *something* coming at them with fiery ears and tail. The long ears glowed eerily . . . the shining tail flicked from side to side like a burning snake. . . .

Never before had the Chiricahuas seen a screaming thing that was all glowing ears and tail. They yelled with fright, then turned and ran. They stumbled over each other to get out of the way. The mescal juice in their brains made the terrible thing look twenty feet tall.

Then J.P. and Bravo were through the howling crowd. Soon they were slipping and sliding down the mountain trail. From behind them came nothing but silence. Even the fiercest Apache warrior dared not follow the awful thing that glowed like a cut-up ghost.

J.P. finally leaped off Bravo's back and led him downhill. The trail became less steep. The boy began to breathe again. Perhaps soon they would reach the desert.

Suddenly another figure blocked their path.

A tall, ugly shape. By the dim starlight J.P. saw the wolf-head mask. *The shaman.* The awful figure moved toward them.

J.P. hurled himself at the shaman. He gripped one arm, felt the figure wince with pain. He struck at it with his fists and suddenly was held in a grip of steel.

With one hand the medicine man reached up and pulled off his long, hideous mask.

J.P. stared. He was afraid to believe what he saw.

"Now take it easy," said the laughing voice. "And tell me fast–how's my ever-loving son J.P.?"

With a great cry of joy the boy leaped up to meet the waiting arms of his father, Donegal Dan.

18

The General's Letter

Together they traveled down the mountain.

To J.P. the trip was a dream; it seemed absolutely unreal. His father spoke very little, but his strong hands were always ready to help when the going became too steep. Then, shortly before daybreak, they found the ruins of a deserted ranch house and decided to wait there for night before traveling farther.

His father now had a small beard. He looked pale and gaunt, and his left arm moved stiffly. Lying in the shade of a cottonwood tree Donegal Dan told of all that had happened to him in the southern desert.

The Apache attack on the government party had been sudden and swift. Only Dan himself had escaped, but not without wounds. A bullet had passed through his left arm and an Apache war club had bruised his skull.

" 'Twas the blow on the head that did the real damage." He grinned at J.P. "My skull split the war club in half. But my good senses were scrambled in the doin'."

Donegal Dan had crawled to a deserted mine. There he found food and water left by the previous owners. But the blow on his head caused him to forget most of his past life. Then there was fever, and long days had passed without memories . . . until one afternoon an Apache stood in the doorway of the ruined mine office.

"Just a boy," his father said. "But with all the courage of a man. And the only one of all those savages able to find me."

Natanah had told him of J.P.'s planned trip to the Apache camp. He had asked for Donegal Dan's help. It was the mention of his son's name that made the scout's memory begin to clear.

After Donegal Dan swore not to betray its location to anyone else, Natanah led him to the Apache camp. There in the tall grass by the fire the white man waited for an opportunity. It came when the shaman left the fire circle to find more mescal juice. Dan grabbed him, tied him up, and changed into his clothes and mask. From then on Dan himself became the medicine man.

"And Quick Killer?" asked J.P. "What happened when he chased the shaman—that is, when he chased after you?"

Donegal Dan grinned. "I purposely made him angry so he *would* chase me. Then I took care of that ferocious gent with a light tap on the jaw. I think his reputation as a warrior will be less than it once was. After all, his friends think he was dropped by an old man without teeth."

His father's eyes glowed. "I'm proud of you, son. Findin' your way to that Apache camp by yourself was no easy trick."

"I only did what you taught me, Dad."

"Then you certainly learned your lessons well."

They rested all day at the deserted ranch house. Bravo, who was now just skin and bones, lay happily in a patch of green bermuda grass and ate until he seemed ready to burst open. Then he yawned and went to sleep—but with one eye open, just in case.

That night they left the ranch house, and the following day they hid again. Now and then they saw an Apache patrol, but none ever came really close. Donegal Dan was too good a scout to leave tracks.

The following evening the three of them reached the familiar adobe hut on the outskirts of Fort Bowie. Donegal Dan paused to rub his chin.

"Too bad I can't shave first," he said wistfully.

J.P.'s eyes twinkled. "I don't think Mamá will mind, Dad."

"Maybe not . . . Now then, son—would you be waitin' a few minutes before comin' inside?"

"You bet."

Donegal Dan walked into the house, and J.P. heard his mother cry out with joy. The wonderful sound brought chills up and down his spine. He hugged Bravo. Together they waited their turn to see Mamacita again.

The following Saturday afternoon there was a party in the big mess hall. Food and drinks were supplied by Big Bull Schultz in honor of his friends, Donegal Dan and J.P.

There was a lake of cream soda for J.P. And there was singing and laughing, and the window-rattling joy of Sergeant Schultz, who sang "Danny Boy" four times in a row until finally someone asked him to please keep quiet.

Everyone was surprised when Colonel Blunt and his wife entered the mess hall. All jumped to attention, but the Colonel quickly waved them to their seats.

"Sergeant Schultz," said the Colonel in a loud voice.

"Yes, sir?"

"Why weren't Mrs. Blunt and myself invited to this party?"

Big Bull swallowed hard. "Begging the Colonel's pardon, sir. But I figured . . ." His voice died away.

"Figured what?"

"Well, sir . . ." He took a deep breath and squared huge shoulders. "Seeing as how the boy is one of two guests of honor, and seeing as how you don't like him—"

"Don't like him!" roared the Colonel. "Foolishness, Sergeant. Of course I like him. In fact, I've been meaning to apologize for that afternoon in my office."

With a smile he held out his hand to J.P. The boy shook it and flushed because everyone was watching them.

"By the way," whispered the Colonel. "Lieutenant Simper apologizes too. Or if he doesn't, he'd better." The commanding officer turned to face the crowd. "Something else, gentlemen. I also came to read a very important letter."

Mrs. Blunt nodded and smiled at J.P.

The Colonel pulled a letter from his pocket. "It's from the Commanding General at Fort Yuma, gentlemen. And it says . . ."

The General congratulated Army Scout Daniel O'Flynn for escaping from the Apaches. The General also wished to congratulate a young man named Juanito O'Flynn whose bravery had been reported to him by the Army stage driver.

"Because of this young man's outstanding character, and because of his keen knowledge of the desert and Indian ways," read the Colonel, "it is the pleasure of the Commanding General to . . ."

Colonel Blunt cleared his throat and looked up. All eyes were on him.

"It is the pleasure of the Commanding General," continued Colonel Blunt, "to appoint Juanito Patrick Mendoza

O'Flynn to the rank of Honorary Scout, United States Sixth Cavalry."

For a moment there was silence. Then a tremendous roar rocked the mess hall. They lifted J.P. high into the air. Way up there he felt prouder than at any time in his life before.

Donegal Dan and Mamacita smiled their pleasure. But suddenly from somewhere in the rear of the mess hall came another kind of sound.

"*Hee-aww . . . Hee-aww . . .*"

And a pale-faced cook in a white, floppy hat ran in from the kitchen. He was holding a saucepan in his right hand.

"Sergeant Schultz, come quick," he spluttered. "A burro has just eaten the officers' salad for tomorrow's meal!"

"You don't say," said Big Bull in a squeaky voice.

"Coming, Sergeant?"

"Of course. That gosh-durned donkey . . ."

He yanked the sauce pan from the cook's hand, gripped it like a weapon, and sped toward the kitchen. Then he stopped. He looked at the pan and handed it back to the cook.

"No need for that, I guess." Big Bull turned and smiled at J.P. "I'll just try and appeal to his dignity."

He walked out and everyone laughed. That is, everyone except J.P. Not that he was worried about Bravo. He had a hunch that from now on his four-legged friend would be able to take dare of himself just fine. No, the reason he didn't laugh was because he was thinking real hard . . .

thinking of how he would tell all this wonderful news to Strong Friend when they met again at the secret place.

His father was home once more, and Mamacita was happier than he had ever seen her before. And J.P. himself was—an honorary scout!

When he finally laughed, he laughed louder than anyone else in the mess hall. Because the Imp was inside his head.

Isn't this a wonderful life? it asked him.

"You bet!" he yelled loudly, then reddened at the sound of his voice.

But Donegal Dan grinned broadly. He knew exactly how J.P. felt.

DATE DUE			
GAYLORD M-2			PRINTED IN U.S.A.

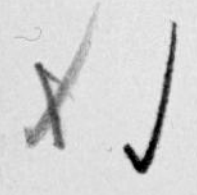